His hand drifted to the middle of her back and pressed lightly.

Sage's own hands rested awkwardly at the sides of his denim jacket. For one brief second, she allowed herself to imagine what it would be like to circle his middle with her arms and nestle fully against him.

Crazy. And highly inappropriate. Certainly not the kind of thoughts a crying woman had about a man.

Except she wasn't crying anymore.

And since her crying had subsided, she really had no reason to keep standing there, snug in Gavin's embrace.

"Sorry about that," she murmured and slowly began to disengage herself.

"Don't be." He halted her by tucking a finger beneath her chin, tilting her head up and bringing his mouth down on hers.

Her arms, no longer awkward and indecisive, clung to him as she gave herself over to what quickly became the most incredible kiss of her life.

Dear Reader,

I consider myself a very fortunate person. One reason is that I live in the foothills of the McDowell Mountains, a gorgeous urban mountain range that borders north Scottsdale. I get to wake up every morning to a spectacular view from my bedroom window and walk my dogs along scenic nature trails that are only minutes away. When I was a teenager, this part of the valley wasn't yet developed, and I used to ride my horse through the same empty desert where I and a thousand of my neighbors now reside. Kind of amazing in a way.

With inspiration like this, I couldn't help but let my mind wander and imagine all sorts of stories blending the past and the present. I'm not quite sure where the idea for *Last Chance Cowboy* came from—it probably occurred to me while driving past the few remaining ranches in the area on my way to the river. But once born, the idea of a wild mustang roaming an urban mountain range quickly took hold, and I couldn't shake it.

I am delighted to bring the story of Gavin, Sage and an amazing horse to you and thrilled to be writing about a place that is both literally and figuratively close to my heart.

Warmest wishes,

Cathy McDavid

P.S. I always enjoy hearing from readers. You can contact me at www.cathymcdavid.com.

Last Chance Cowboy

CATHY McDAVID

TORONTO NEW YORK LONDON
AMSTERDAM PARIS SYDNEY HAMBURG
STOCKHOLM ATHENS TOKYO MILAN MADRID
PRAGUE WARSAW BUDAPEST AUCKLAND

Recycling programs
for this product may
not exist in your area.

ISBN-13: 978-0-373-75369-7

LAST CHANCE COWBOY

Copyright © 2011 by Cathy McDavid

Printed in U.S.A.

ABOUT THE AUTHOR

Cathy makes her home in Scottsdale, Arizona, near the breathtaking McDowell Mountains where hawks fly overhead, javelina traipse across her front yard and mountain lions occasionally come calling. She embraced the country life at an early age, acquiring her first horse in eighth grade. Dozens of horses followed through the years, along with mules, an obscenely fat donkey, chickens, ducks, goats and a pot-bellied pig who had her own swimming pool. Nowadays, two spoiled dogs and two spoiled-er cats round out the McDavid pets. Cathy loves contemporary and historical ranch stories and often incorporates her own experiences into her books.

When not writing, Cathy and her family and friends spend as much time as they can at her cabin in the small town of Young. Of course, she takes her laptop with her on the chance inspiration strikes.

Books by Cathy McDavid

HARLEQUIN AMERICAN ROMANCE

1168—HIS ONLY WIFE
1197—THE FAMILY PLAN*
1221—COWBOY DAD
1264—WAITING FOR BABY
1294—TAKING ON TWINS*
1307—THE ACCIDENTAL SHERIFF*
1318—DUSTY: WILD COWBOY
1345—THE COMEBACK COWBOY

*Fatherhood

Chapter One

The trail, narrow and steep, all but disappeared as it wrapped around the sheer mountain ledge. Good thing heights didn't bother him, Gavin Powell thought as his horse's hoof slipped and sent a shower of rocks tumbling to the ravine bottom forty feet below. He loosened his reins, giving the paint mare her head. She was small but sure-footed and carefully picked her way along the ledge with the concentration of a tightrope walker.

This wasn't a trail for novices—not one on which Gavin took the customers of his family's riding stable. He'd discovered the trail as a teenager over fifteen years ago and rode it every now and then when he craved peace and solitude.

Shaking his head, he chuckled dismally. Who'd have ever thought he'd need to retreat to this remote trail in order to find solitude? Not Gavin. Until a few years ago, their nearest neighbors had been fifteen miles down a single lane road that saw little traffic. Now, their nearest neighbors were at the end of the long drive leading from what little remained of Powell Ranch.

All nine hundred of them.

Gavin pushed away the thought. He'd come here to relax and unwind, not work himself into a sweat. Besides, if he was going to expend large amounts of mental and emotional energies, it would be on one of his many pressing personal problems, not something he was powerless to change.

The mare abruptly stopped, balancing on a precipice no wider than her shoulders. Gavin had to tuck his left arm close to his side or rub the sleeve of his denim jacket against the rugged rock face.

"Come on, Shasta." He nudged the mare gently. "Now's not the time to lose your courage."

She raised her head but remained rooted in place, her ears twitching slightly and her round eyes staring out across the ravine.

Rather than nudge her again, Gavin reached for the binoculars he carried in his saddlebags, only to realize he'd forgotten to bring them along. Pushing back the brim of his cowboy hat, he squinted against the glaring noonday sun, searching the peaks and gullies. The mare obviously sensed something, and he trusted her instincts more than he trusted his own.

All at once, she tensed and let out a shrill whinny, her sides quivering.

"What do you see, girl?"

Shasta snorted in reply.

Gavin continued scanning the rugged mountain terrain. Just as he was ready to call it quits, he spotted movement across the ravine. A black shape traveled down the steep slope, zig-zagging between towering saguaro cacti and prickly cholla. Too dark for a mule deer, too large for a coyote and too fast for a human, the shape could be only one thing.

The wild mustang!

He reached again for his saddlebags, but he'd forgotten his camera, too. Dammit. Well, he really didn't need another picture. Especially one from such a far distance. He'd already taken dozens of the mustang, many of which he'd sent to the U.S. Bureau of Land Management when he'd first spotted the horse. All he'd received in response was a polite letter thanking him for the information and giving a weak assurance they would investigate the matter.

That was June. It was now October.

The BLM probably figured the horse was an escapee from one of the residents in Mustang Village, the community now occupying the land once belonging to Gavin's family. Or that the horse had crossed over from the Indian reservation on the other side of the McDowell Mountains. The last wild mustangs left this part of Arizona more than sixty years ago, or so the stories his grandfather used to tell him went. As a teenager, his grandfather had rounded up wild mustangs. No way could this horse be one of them.

But Gavin's heart told him different. Maybe, by some miracle, one descendant had survived.

Gavin was going to capture him. He'd made the decision two months ago when yet another phone call to the BLM yielded absolutely nothing. Even if the horse was simply an escapee, it was in danger from injuries, illness, ranchers not opposed to shooting a wild horse, and possibly predators, though mountain lions in this area were a rarity these days.

He told himself his intentions were selfless—he was thinking only of the horse's safety and well-being.

Truthfully, Gavin wanted the horse for himself. As a tribute. To his grandfather and to the cowboy way of life he loved, which was disappearing bit by bit every day. Then, he would breed the mustang to his mares, many of which, like Shasta, had bloodlines going all the way back to the wild mustangs of his grandfather's time.

He'd recently acquired a partner with deep pockets, a man from Mustang Valley, and developed a business plan. All he needed was the stud horse.

This weekend, he, his partner, his brother and their two ranch hands would go out. By Monday, if all went well, Gavin's family would have a new revenue stream, and the years of barely making ends meet would be forever behind them.

All at once, the black spot vanished, swallowed by the uneven terrain.

Gavin reached for his saddlebag a third time and pulled out a map, marking the location and date. Later tonight, he would add the information to the log he kept tracking the mustang's travels.

"Let's go, girl."

With another lusty snort, Shasta continued along the ledge as if nothing out of the ordinary had happened. Her metal shoes clinked on the hard boulders beneath her feet. In the sky above, a pair of redtail hawks rode the wind currents as they searched for prey.

An hour later, Gavin and Shasta reached the main trail that traversed the northern section of the McDowell Sonoran Preserve. It was along here that Gavin and his brother guided their customers. Most of the horse-owning residents of Mustang Village favored the gently winding trail, where four generations of Powells had driven their cattle after spring and fall roundups.

Gavin hated thinking there wouldn't be a fifth generation.

As he neared his family's villa, with its large barn and adjoining stables, his gaze automatically wandered to the valley below, and he was struck with yet another pang of nostalgia. Not long ago, Powell cattle had roamed the open range, feeding on the lush vegetation that grew along a small branch of the Salt River.

These days, houses, apartments and commercial buildings took the place of open range, and the river had been dammed up to create an urban lake and surrounding park.

Gavin understood that progress couldn't be stopped. He just wished it hadn't come to Mustang Valley.

Dismounting, he waved to the adult students taking riding lessons in the main arena. Later, after the grade school let out for the day, the equestrian drill team would practice their routines there.

He'd given up hope that his twelve-year-old daughter, Cassie, would become a member. Not that she didn't like horses. Quite the opposite. She spent most of her free time in the stables, and for someone who'd never ridden until this past summer, she'd taken to it like a natural. Apparently there was something to be said for genes.

No, the reason his daughter wouldn't join the school equestrian team was the same reason she had few real friends and was struggling with her classes.

Slow to fit in, Principal Rodgers liked to say, despite scoring high on her placement tests. The move from Connecticut to Arizona was a big adjustment. As was switching from private school to public school. So was living full-time with her mom to living full-time with a dad she hardly knew.

The adjustments weren't easy for his sensitive and often emotional daughter.

Leading Shasta into the stables, he tethered her to a hitching rail outside the tack room, unsaddled her and proceeded to give her a good brushing. He heard a familiar whistling and glanced up to see Ethan approaching, his farrier chaps slung low on his hips. A casual observer might not notice the limp, which had improved considerably in the ten months since his discharge from the Marines.

Gavin noticed, however, and winced inwardly every time he thought of the injury that had permanently disabled his younger brother.

"You have a visitor," Ethan announced, coming to stand by Gavin and resting a forearm on the mare's hind quarters. "A lady visitor."

Gavin's stomach instantly tightened. "Not Principal Rodgers again?"

Ethan's eyes sparked with undisguised curiosity. "This gal's about thirty years younger than Principal Rodgers. And a lot better looking."

"Someone from town?" Though Mustang Village was technically a residential community, Gavin and his family always referred to it as a town.

"I don't think so. She doesn't have the look."

"An attorney?" He wouldn't put it past Cassie's mother to serve him with papers despite their recently revised joint-custody agreement.

"No. She's a cowgirl for sure. Pulled in with a truck and trailer."

Gavin knew he should quit stalling and just go meet the woman. But given the family's run of bad luck in recent years, he tended to anticipate the worst whenever visitors wouldn't identify themselves.

"Got a girlfriend on the side you haven't mentioned?" Ethan's mouth lifted in an amused grin.

"When's the last time you saw me on a date?"

"If you're considering it, you could do worse than this gal."

Gavin refused to acknowledge his brother's remark. "Where's she waiting?"

"In the living room. With Cassie."

He ground his teeth together. "Couldn't you have stayed with her and sent Cassie instead?"

"She'll be fine. Your daughter isn't half the trouble you think she is."

"Yeah, tell that to Principal Rodgers." Gavin pushed the brush he'd been using into his brother's hand. "Take care of Shasta for me, will you?"

Without waiting for an answer, he started down the stable

aisle. As he entered the open area in front of the main arena, he dusted off his jeans, removed his hat and combed his fingers through his hair. Passing two of his adult students, he nodded and murmured, "Afternoon." He might not like people living in the valley once owned by his family and traipsing all over his property, but without their business, he and his family would lose their only source of income.

At the kitchen door, he kicked the toes of his boots against the threshold, dislodging any dust before entering the house. A tantalizing aroma greeted him, and he turned to see a pot of spaghetti sauce simmering on the old gas range. His father's doing. Since Gavin's mother died, cooking was the only chore on the ranch Wayne Powell did with any regularity.

The sound of voices carried from the other room, one of them Cassie's. Did she know this woman?

Gavin's anxiety increased. He disliked surprises.

His footsteps on the Saltillo tile floor must have alerted Cassie and the woman because they were both facing him when he entered the old house's spacious living room.

"Hi." He removed his hat and, after a brief second of indecision, set it on the coffee table. "I'm Gavin Powell."

The woman stepped and greeted him with a pleasant smile. "Sage Navarre."

He shook her extended hand, appreciating her firm grip. Ethan had been right. Ms. Navarre was definitely attractive, her Hispanic heritage evident in her brown eyes and darker brown hair, pulled back in a sleek ponytail. Her jeans were loose and faded, and her Western-cut shirt functional. Yet there was no disguising the feminine curves hiding beneath the clothing.

"What can I do for you?" he asked, noticing that Cassie observed him closely, her new puppy cradled in her arms. One of the ranch dogs had delivered a litter a few months ago, and Gavin had told her she could keep one. The pair had been inseparable ever since.

"I'm from the BLM," Ms. Navarre said, as if that alone explained everything.

A jolt shot through Gavin. "The BLM?"

"Bureau of Land Management." She held up the leather jacket she'd been carrying, showing him the badge pinned to the front, then handed him a business card. "Aren't you the person who contacted us about a feral horse in the area?"

"Yes." He glanced only briefly at the card, then spoke carefully. "I assumed from the lack of response, you folks weren't taking me seriously."

"Well, we are. I'm here to round up the horse and transport him to our facility in Show Low."

Cassie's expression brightened. "Cool."

"I'll need your cooperation, of course," Ms. Navarre added. "And a stall to board my horse, if you have one available."

"I'm sorry, Ms. Navarre." Gavin returned her card to her. He had too much invested in the horse to forfeit ownership just because some woman from the BLM showed up out of the blue. And he sure as hell wasn't going to help her. "I'm afraid you've wasted your time coming here."

"I DON'T UNDERSTAND." Sage studied Gavin Powell, admittedly confused. "Is there a problem?"

"I've changed my mind."

"About?"

"The horse. *I'm* going to capture him and keep him."

She may have only just met him, but there was no mistaking the fierce set of his jaw and the steel in his voice. Here stood a man with a mission and the determination to carry it out.

Unfortunately, he was about to come up against a brick wall.

"You can't, Mr. Powell," she stated firmly.

"Why not?"

"It's against the law for anyone other than an employee of the BLM to capture a feral horse."

"The McDowell Sonoran Preserve isn't federal land."

"No. But it isn't private land, either." She bent and placed her business card on a hand-carved pine coffee table. "And besides, the law isn't restricted to federal land. If you capture the horse, you'd be in violation of the law and subject to fines and a possible jail sentence."

His jaw went from being set to working furiously.

Stubborn, she concluded. Or was he angry? Another glance at him confirmed the latter.

Sage's defenses rose. "I realize you had other plans for the horse, but you knew I was coming."

"No, I didn't."

"We called. Last week."

"I received no phone call."

"It's noted in the records. I don't have the name of the individual we spoke to offhand, but I can easily obtain it if you give me a minute."

He glanced at the girl—Cassie, wasn't it?—and his gaze narrowed.

"Don't look at me," she protested, a hint of defiance in the downward turn of her mouth.

Not that Sage was good at determining ages, but Gavin Powell didn't appear old enough to be Cassie's father. Sage guessed him to be around her own thirty-one years. Maybe older. Rugged and tanned complexions like his could be misleading.

Broad shoulders and well-muscled forearms also spoke of a life dedicated to hard physical labor and being outdoors. She'd always found that kind of man attractive. One who rode a horse or swung a hammer or chopped trees rather than earning his pay from behind a desk.

Gavin Powell exemplified that type, with the glaring addition of a very testy and confrontational personality. Something she *didn't* find attractive.

Sage stood straighter. She'd come to Powell Ranch on business, after all. Not to check out the available men.

"Is it possible someone else took the call and didn't tell you?" she asked.

"Not likely."

"Grandpa forgets to tell you stuff all the time," Cassie interjected.

"Go do your homework," Gavin told her.

"I hardly have any. I did most of it in class."

"Now."

"Dad!"

Her cajoling had no effect on him. At a stern "Cassie," she exited the room, another flash of defiance in her eyes.

So, the girl *was* his daughter. No sooner did Sage wonder how often those exchanges happened than she reminded herself it was none of her concern.

"Sorry about that," he mumbled when his daughter had gone.

For a tiny moment, he appeared human. And vulnerable.

"I have a daughter, too," she admitted, "though she's only six."

Why in the world had she told him that? She rarely discussed Isa when on the job. It was easier when dealing with obstinate or difficult individuals—an unfortunate and commonplace occurrence in her job—to keep the discussions impersonal.

She promptly brought the subject back around. "Look, Mr. Powell. I'm here to capture the horse, which can't be allowed to wander on state and city land. I'd like your help."

His scowl deepened. Heck, maybe it was permanent.

"To be honest," she said, making a civil plea, "I really need it. You know this area, I don't. And from the information you sent the BLM, you've clearly been tracking the horse."

"No." He shook his head. A lock of jet-black hair fell over his forehead. He pushed it back with an impatient swipe. "I want the mustang, Ms. Navarre. I won't help you."

"If you persist in capturing him yourself, I'll report you to the authorities."

"No kidding?" The challenge in his tone told her she would have to go that far, and perhaps further, to obtain his cooperation.

Sage released a frustrated sigh. Her tidy plan was unraveling at an alarming rate. A few days, a week at the most, was all the time she had to capture the horse. Then, as she and her boss had agreed, she'd spend her annual two weeks' vacation in nearby Scottsdale visiting her cousin. It was the main reason she'd asked to be assigned to this case—locating and confronting her errant ex with her attorney cousin-in-law at her side.

After four years, she'd finally gotten a reliable lead on her ex's whereabouts, and it had brought her to Mustang Village. The back child support he owed her—owed *Isa*—amounted to a considerable sum of money. Well worth two weeks of vacation and scrambling to rearrange both her and her daughter's schedules.

Much as she hated admitting it, she couldn't capture the horse without Gavin Powell's help and his resources. Not in one week. Probably not ever.

She could try for an order, but that would require time she didn't have. Besides, the task would go quicker and easier with his voluntary cooperation.

Sage thought fast. She was a field agent, her job was to safely capture wild horses and burros. Once in federal custody, the adoption of those horses and burros was handled by a different department. She knew a few people in that department and was confident she could pull a few strings.

"What if, in exchange for your help, I guaranteed you ownership of the horse?"

Gavin Powell studied her skeptically. "Can you do that?"

She lowered herself onto the couch, the well-worn leather cushions giving gently beneath her weight. She imagined, like the coffee table, the dated but well-constructed couch had been in the Powell family a long time.

"Can we sit a minute? I've had a long drive."

He joined her with obvious reluctance and, rather than recline, sat stiffly with a closed fist resting on his knee.

She'd almost rather face a pair of flailing front hooves—something she'd done more than once in the course of her job.

"The fact is, Mr. Powell, we have trouble finding enough homes for the animals we round up. Despite the novelty of owning a feral horse or burro, most people aren't interested in spending months and months domesticating them. Even then, some animals never truly adapt, and only a handful of the horses make decent and dependable riding stock."

"I wouldn't be using the horse for riding."

Though she was curious, she didn't ask about his intentions for the horse. "I think the BLM would be happy to have a home for the mustang and will likely just give him to you with a minimal amount of paperwork and processing."

He nodded contemplatively.

"You'd still have to pay a fee."

"How much?"

"I don't know for certain. I can find out if you want. Most of the horses are adopted for a few hundred dollars. My guess is it would be something in that range."

Another nod. Gavin Powell was clearly a man of few words.

"I have one week to round up the horse. After that, I'll be staying in Scottsdale with relatives until the end of the month. My daughter's there now, I dropped her off on the way." She paused, giving herself a mental shake. Why did she feel the need to rattle off personal information? "If you don't object, the horse can stay here with you on your ranch while I'm in Scottsdale. You'll have a chance to observe him, work with him, see if he…meets your needs."

She waited while he mulled over her proposition. He didn't take long to make his decision.

"Deal." He extended his hand.

"Good. Glad that's resolved."

Shaking his hand for the second time that afternoon, she tried to hide her relief. Like before, she noticed both strength and assurance in his callused fingers. Gavin Powell was *definitely* one of those men who didn't make his living sitting behind a desk.

"Would you like something in writing?" She asked. "I can have the office fax—"

"Not necessary. I was raised to take someone at their word. And not to give mine unless I intend to keep it."

She didn't doubt that. "Then we're in agreement."

"Yes, ma'am."

"Please, call me Sage. We're going to be working together, after all."

"Gavin."

She smiled.

So did he. And though reserved, it both transformed him and disarmed her. She hadn't noticed his vivid blue eyes or the pleasingly masculine lines of his face until now.

For a moment, Sage lost track of her thoughts. Standing, she promptly gathered them.

"About that stall for my mare."

"Sure." He also stood. "You can pull your truck around to the stables and unload her there."

"Any chance I can park my trailer here? My cousin's home-owners association won't allow me to leave it there."

"No problem."

They went through the back of the house rather than the front door where Sage had entered. She caught a whiff of something tantalizing when they entered the kitchen, reminding her that all she'd eaten since breakfast was a semistale leftover doughnut and a snack-size box of raisins Isa must have accidentally left in her purse.

A man stood at the stove, stirring a pot. He turned and before Gavin introduced the man, she recognized the resemblance.

"Dad, this is Sage Navarre. From the BLM. My dad, Wayne."

"The BLM?" Confusion clouded Wayne Powell's face, then abruptly cleared. "Oh. Yeah. I forgot. Someone called last week."

"That's what I heard."

To Gavin's credit, if he was annoyed at his father, he didn't let on. There was no point anyway; they'd reached an agreement about the horse.

"Nice to meet you, Ms. Navarre."

"Sage," she told Gavin's father.

"Will you be in Mustang Valley long?"

"A week at the most."

"We'd better tend to that mare of yours," Gavin said, inclining his head toward the door.

Sage got the hint. Gavin didn't wish to prolong the conversation with his father. "It was a pleasure, Mr. Powell."

"Enjoy your stay. I hope to see you again." He smiled, but it was mechanical and flat. Nothing like his son's.

"I'm counting on it," she answered cheerfully, and followed Gavin outside.

"I'll meet you in front of the stables," he told her.

They parted, and Sage headed toward her truck. As she drove the short distance to the stables, she caught sight of Cassie watching from the back porch, her form partially obscured by a thick wooden column.

Without thinking, Sage waved. Cassie ducked her head behind the column, then reappeared a second later, waving shyly in return.

An interesting family, Sage mused, though a little unusual. She supposed there was a lot more to them than met the eye.

Pulling up in front of the stables, she reminded herself why she was in Mustang Valley: capture the wild horse and collect four years' worth of back child support from her ex.

Any distractions, most especially those in the form of a good-looking cowboy, were counterproductive. Not to mention inviting trouble.

Chapter Two

Gavin waited as Sage unlatched the trailer door and swung it wide. He expected the horse to bolt backward as most did after a long ride. Not so this one. The mare lifted her left rear foot and placed it gingerly down, as if not quite believing solid ground awaited. Her right rear foot followed, then the rest of her compact and sturdy body emerged inch by inch. Once standing on all fours, she turned her head with the regality of a visiting dignitary and surveyed her new surroundings.

"She's a good-looking horse." In fact, Gavin had never seen one with that same charcoal-gray coloring.

"Her name's Avaro." Sage reached under the mare's impressively long mane to stroke her neck. "It's Spanish for *greedy*. And trust me, it fits. She attacks every meal like it's her last."

"A mustang?"

"She was brought in on a roundup about three years ago in the Four Corners area. I had another horse at the time, a good one. But as soon as I saw Avaro, I wanted her."

Gavin could appreciate that. He felt the same about his mustang.

"Not just because of her coat," Sage continued, "though it's pretty unusual."

"She'd make a nice broodmare." He was thinking of his own mares, the ones with mustang bloodlines.

Sage shrugged. "Maybe someday. Right now, I'm using her too much and too hard."

"How long did it take you to break her?"

"Six months." Sage laughed, her brown eyes filling with memories.

"That long?"

"It was weeks before she let me near her. Another month before I could put a halter on her."

Gavin considered the information. He'd been hoping to start breeding the mustang stallion right away. Might be difficult if he couldn't even get a halter on the horse. "Your perseverance paid off."

"I told you, owning a feral horse isn't easy."

"I'm up to the task."

She studied him with a critical eye. "I believe you are."

The compliment, if indeed it was one, pleased him.

They started toward the stables with Sage leading Avaro, who observed everything with large intelligent eyes. It was that intelligence that had enabled her to survive by her wits in what had been a harsh and dangerous world. It was a quality he hoped to produce in his foals.

At the entrance to the stables, they heard a familiar rhythmic clinking.

"Do you think your farrier could have a look at Avaro's right front hoof?" Sage asked. "Her shoe's a little loose, and I don't want any problems when we head out into the mountains."

"That's my brother, Ethan. As a rule, he only works on our horses, but I'm sure I could ask him to make an exception."

"If there's a local farrier—"

"It's all right. Our regular guy's usually booked several days out. We may not be able to get him here until after the weekend, and I know you don't want to wait that long."

"No, I don't," she agreed.

Gavin didn't explain the reasons his brother only shoed

their own horses. Farrier work was physically demanding and hard on Ethan's prosthetic leg.

Fixing a single loose shoe, however, wasn't nearly as strenuous. And like Sage, Gavin didn't want to postpone capturing the wild mustang any longer than necessary. Business tended to slow down during the holidays. He wanted his stud and breeding operation well underway before then.

"You have a great setup," Sage said appreciatively.

"Thanks."

"How long has the ranch been here?"

At one time telling the history of his family's ranch had been a source of pride. No more. Not after the past ten years. But because she was being friendly, he answered her question.

"My great-grandfather Abe Powell built the original house and stables after he moved here from Texas. According to my grandfather, he was evading the law."

"Is it true?"

"I don't know. But it makes for a good story."

"When was that?"

"Right before the turn of the century. *Last* century. The house wasn't much more than a shack. The stable consisted of six standing stalls and one box stall."

"You've added on since then." She smiled.

It was, Gavin observed, a nice smile. Open and honest.

"For thirty years, we had the only cattle operation in the area. Before he died, my great-grandfather was able to build the villa, the barn, the bunkhouse and expand the stables. We have thirty-two box stalls now. No standing stalls. And six pens out back along with three connecting two-acre pastures."

Gavin stopped at an empty stall not far from where his brother worked on a large gelding. He unlatched the stall door, and Sage led her mare inside.

"My office will reimburse you the cost of boarding Avaro."

"I'll draw up an invoice." He would have liked to tell her not to worry about it. But with six empty stalls, they could use the extra income.

They stood with forearms resting on the stall wall, watching Avaro acquaint herself with her new accommodations.

"With that much cattle, your family must own quite a bit of land."

"We used to. Six hundred acres. All of Mustang Valley, which is now Mustang Village."

"Wow!"

He swore he could see the wheels in her head spinning as she mentally calculated the huge chunk of change they must have received when they sold the land.

What she didn't know was that every dime had been spent on his mother's heart transplant and medical care. So much money. Sadly, it had bought her only another few months of life before her body rejected the replacement heart, and she died of severe infection. Even if there had been money for a second transplant, the doctors weren't able to save her.

"We kept about thirty acres."

"I'm surprised you didn't move," Sage said.

"Powell Ranch is my home. My family's lived here for four generations." He went to bed every night praying there would be a fifth. "And while most of the land is developed, the ranch is still the heart of this valley."

She looked at him. Really looked at him. Intently. As if she was trying to read what lay hidden beneath the surface.

Gavin turned away. He didn't want Sage, or anyone for that matter, seeing how deeply affected he was by his loss.

WITH AVARO SETTLED AND snacking hungrily on some grain, Gavin took Sage over to meet his brother. Two of the ranch's several dogs lay curled together by the tack room door, their heads resting on their paws and their wagging tails stirring up small dust clouds in the dirt.

Ethan slowly straightened, letting go of the gelding's hoof he'd had braced between his knees. "Hi, again." Setting his rasp on top of his toolbox, he removed his gloves and stuffed them in the waistband of his chaps.

"Ethan, this is Sage Navarre," Gavin said. "She's with the BLM."

"Really?" He wiped the back of his hand across his brow, which had risen in surprise. "Is this about the mustang?"

"Yes."

Ethan's glance cut to Gavin.

"Sage is here to capture the mustang, and we're going to help her."

"We are?"

"She says the BLM will allow me to purchase him and bypass the usual adoption process."

"That's great." Ethan's features relaxed into a grin. "Glad to hear it."

"Her mare has a loose shoe. Any chance you can check it out when you're done with Baldy here?"

"Happy to." Ethan stepped forward, his leg wobbling for a second before he steadied it.

"No rush," Gavin said.

Ethan responded to the concern in Gavin's voice. "I'll handle it." To Sage, he said, "How long you staying?"

They chatted amicably for a few minutes. Well, Sage and Ethan chatted amicably. Gavin mostly listened. And observed. While he'd struck a deal with Sage, he wasn't a hundred percent sure of her. Then again, to be honest, he was betting his future stud and breeding operation on his new partner, a man he didn't know a whole lot better than her.

Gavin wished he weren't so desperate. Normally, he proceeded far more cautiously.

"You ready to park your trailer?" he asked during a break in the conversation.

After a word of advice about Avaro's tendency to nip, Sage followed Gavin.

Outside the stables, she paused. "Which way?"

"I'll ride with you. It'll be easier than trying to give you directions."

The inside of her truck was messy. Crayons, coloring books, dolls, a stuffed cat and a collection of tiny farm animals occupied the passenger seat. A notebook, travel log, empty paper cup, a CD case and a partially folded map filled the middle. Unidentifiable trash littered the floor.

"Sorry about the mess," Sage said, sweeping her daughter's toys into the pile of her things. "Isa gets bored on road trips. I'm sure you understand."

"Not really."

Her apologetic smile fell.

Ignoring the well-deserved stab of guilt, Gavin climbed into the passenger seat, his feet inadvertently kicking the trash. He'd already told Sage more about his family than he intended. Cassie was off-limits.

"That way," he said, and pointed, acutely aware of the tension his remark had created.

Sage said nothing, leaving Gavin to stew silently. How could he explain to Sage, a virtual stranger, that he'd only seen his daughter a few times while she was growing up? That money for plane trips to Connecticut was hard to spare. In December, he and Cassie's mother would revisit the full custody issue. If Cassie wasn't happy, wasn't adjusting to school, if her and Gavin's relationship didn't improve, she might be returning to Connecticut. Given the current state of his family's finances, he had no idea when he'd be able to swing another visit.

Not a day passed Gavin didn't stare his many failures as a father square in the face and wish circumstances were different.

Picking up the stuffed cat, he set it on top of the coloring book. "Cassie's kind of a neat freak. Always has been."

His explanation appeared to appease Sage for her features softened. "You don't know how lucky you are."

Except he did know. This six-month trial he had with Cassie had been an unexpected gift. The result of her mother's recent remarriage and pregnancy. He hated that he hadn't immediately formed a close bond with Cassie, one like Sage and her daughter obviously shared. And he worried constantly that he'd lose Cassie before he ever really had her.

"Pull into the barn," he told Sage. "That way, you can park in the shade."

"Wow. You really did have some cattle operation." Her gaze roamed the interior of the large barn. "I'm impressed."

"Most of the equipment's gone." They'd sold it off piece by piece over the years.

"Yeah, but it wouldn't take much to start up again." Sage rotated the crank on the hitch, lowering the trailer's front end.

Gavin went around to the rear of the trailer and placed the blocks of wood she'd given him behind the tires. "My plans are to turn it into a mare motel."

"Really?" He could see she'd deduced his plans for the wild mustang. "It would make a good one."

Gavin wondered if he should be less leery of Sage. She seemed genuinely nice and willing to make their agreement work.

"What time tomorrow are we starting?" She shut and locked the trailer's storage compartment.

"We can't head out until Saturday."

"Oh."

"I wasn't expecting you. My day's full."

"Okay." Disappointment showed in her face.

"I do have a free hour in the afternoon. Maybe you can come by. We'll go over the maps and logs and decide on the best area to start looking."

"Sounds good. Any chance I can bring my daughter? She loves horses. I keep promising to buy her a pony of her own and teach her to ride one of these days but just haven't had the time."

"We've got a dead broke horse we use for beginner students. She can ride him if she wants." Gavin had no idea why he made the offer.

"Thank you. That's very nice of you." Her smile returned, brighter than before.

Maybe that was why.

As they were climbing back into the truck, her cell phone rang. She lifted it out of the cup holder and, with only a cursory glance at the screen, answered.

"Hi. I just finished parking my trailer." A long pause followed during which she listened intently, her mouth pursed in concentration. "Yeah, hold on a second." She dug through the pile in the middle of the seat, locating a notebook. "Go ahead." She wrote something down that appeared to be directions, though Gavin couldn't see clearly from where he sat in the passenger seat. "Great. Meet you in fifteen minutes."

Snapping the notebook closed, she started the truck. "I'm sorry to be so abrupt, but I have to leave."

"No problem. Three o'clock tomorrow okay? To meet here," he added when she didn't immediately respond.

"Oh, yeah." She shook her head as if to clear it. "Three o'clock."

After she dropped Gavin off in front of the house, he stood

for a moment watching her truck bump down the long sloping driveway leading to the main road.

Apparently she knew someone in Mustang Village.

He didn't like that his curiosity was piqued. He liked the anticipation he felt at seeing her again tomorrow even less.

SAGE REACHED THE BASE of the mountain and merged with the light traffic traveling east. A quarter mile up the road, she spotted a stone sign marking the main entrance to Mustang Village. Next to the sign stood a life-size and very realistic bronze statue of a rearing horse.

Just inside the entrance was a modest shopping plaza with retail stores, a bank, fresh food market, urgent care center and two restaurants, one fast-food, one sit-down. Situated behind the shopping plaza was a commercial building with offices on the first floor and apartments on the second. Stretching beyond that were acres and acres of houses as far as she could see.

What had it been like when all this was once an endless rolling valley at the base of a scenic mountain range? She could almost envision it in her mind's eye.

Gavin's family had probably made a killing when they sold the land, but Sage wasn't sure she could have traded glorious and primitive desert for a sea of commercial and residential development.

A second sign directed her to the visitors' center. She turned into the parking lot, shut off the ignition and, as instructed, waited for her cousin's husband.

As the minutes dragged by, Sage's nervousness increased. She tried distracting herself by observing life at midafternoon in Mustang Village.

It was, she had to agree, a unique and almost genius blending of country life and town life. Cars drove by at a very safe fifteen miles per hour while an empty school bus returned from delivering children home. Exercise enthusiasts walked or jogged or biked along the sidewalks, and people on horseback rode the designated bridle paths networking the community. As the warning signs posted everywhere stated, horses had the right of way in Mustang Village.

Finally, just when Sage was ready to get out of her truck and start pacing, her cousin's husband arrived, his SUV slipping into the space beside hers.

She greeted him with a relieved hug. He'd been at work when she stopped by their house earlier to drop off Isa, so she'd yet to see him.

"Thank you, Roberto," she told him when they broke apart. "You have no idea how much I appreciate this."

"Happy to help, *primita*."

Calling her "little cousin" always made Sage smile. At five-eight, he was no more than an inch taller than her. When she wore boots, like today, they stood nose to nose.

Not so with Gavin Powell. Even in boots, she'd had to tilt her head back in order to meet those vivid blue eyes of his.

Why had she thought of him all of a sudden?

"We'd better get a move on," Roberto said. "Before he figures out you're in the area and takes off."

"You have the paperwork?" she asked, hopping in the passenger side of his SUV.

"Right here." Roberto tapped the front of his suit jacket.

He'd used his firm's resources to locate Sage's ex—*again*. This time, she assured herself, would be different. Dan wouldn't be able to disappear before they had a chance to personally serve him with the child support demand papers.

She marveled at his ability to jump from place to place, always one step ahead of her. As a horse trainer, a good one, he easily found work all over the Southwest. He was also often paid in cash or by personal check, which had made garnishing his wages nearly impossible.

To her knowledge, this was the first time he'd returned to Arizona in two years.

"He sure picked a nice spot," she observed, taking in the attractive houses with their tidy front yards, each landscaped with natural desert fauna to conserve water. The homes sat on three-quarter acre lots, with small corrals and shaded pens visible in the spacious backyards.

"*Very* nice," Roberto concurred. "And Mustang Village is teeming with horse people, a lot of them with surplus money and a burning desire for their kids to have the best-trained horses. Dan's probably doing pretty well for himself."

"He always has." That was something Sage didn't understand. Her ex could afford the child support. He just refused to pay it.

Another thing Sage didn't understand was his disinterest in seeing Isa. How could a father who'd been devoted to his daughter for the first two years of her life not want to see her? Spend time with her? Be a vital part of her growing up?

"We're here," Roberto said, and maneuvered the SUV into the driveway of a large Santa Fe–style house.

"Do you think he's home?" Sage asked, her worry spiking at the noticeable absence of a vehicle in the driveway.

Roberto grinned confidently. "Only one way to find out."

At Dan's front door, Roberto rung the bell.

Sage read the hand-painted stone plaque hanging beside the door.

The Rivera Family.

His last name, penned with large, bold strokes, reminded her that she and Dan had never married. She'd wanted to, had brought up the subject frequently during their three years together, but Dan had always manufactured some excuse.

Roberto rang the doorbell again. Sage rubbed her sweaty palms on the front of her jeans.

The Rivera Family.

Suddenly it struck her. Family! As in wife and children.

Before her thought had a chance to fully develop, the door swung open, and Dan appeared in the frame, his expectant expression dissolving into a frown the instant he spotted her.

"What do you want, Sage?"

"To make sure you receive a copy of this." Roberto attempted to hand Dan the child support demand letter. "Since you haven't responded to the nine previous ones mailed to you."

He drew back, refusing to accept the papers. "Who the hell are you?"

"Ms. Navarre's attorney."

"Get off my property."

"You owe my client four years of back child support. You can't get out of it just because—"

"Dan, who is it?" A young, strikingly beautiful and very pregnant woman appeared behind Dan, a toddler boy balanced on her hip.

"It's okay, Maria," he said crossly. "I have this handled."

She backed away, a mixture of confusion and concern on her face, then disappeared into the house's dim interior.

The sudden realization that Dan had committed to another woman when he'd refused to commit to her stung bitterly. It shouldn't, Sage told herself. She was over him. Past that. Moved on. And yet, her heart broke like a dam, releasing fresh pain.

Just then, Dan's cell phone rang. Angling his body away from them, he answered it, speaking in clipped, short sentences. "Hello. Yeah. Not today. Look, Gavin, I'm busy right now. Call you later."

Alarm shot through Sage, leaving her unsteady.

Was that Gavin Powell calling Dan?

She took a deep breath, only vaguely aware of Roberto

whispering to her that they weren't leaving until they'd served Dan with the papers.

Slowly, rationality returned. Gavin had no idea Dan was Isa's father. He owned the local riding stables, and Dan was a horse trainer. It stood to reason they knew each other and possibly had dealings together. Clients in common.

Dan disconnected and, pocketing his cell phone, turned back around. "As I was saying—"

"As *I* was saying…" Roberto tried again to give Dan the papers.

He swatted them away. "You're not getting anything from me without proof."

"Proof of what, Dan?" Sage demanded, her voice shaking from residual shock and rising anger.

"Paternity. How do I even know Isa's mine?"

Sage reeled as if physically struck. "Of course she's yours," she sputtered.

"I'm not so sure. You were still seeing that old boyfriend of yours."

"We worked together. That's all."

"Yeah? Well, get the kid tested. Then we'll talk." With that, Dan slammed the door in Sage's and Roberto's faces.

Chapter Three

Gavin opened his front door to a miniature version of Sage, complete with boots, jeans and a floppy cowboy hat.

"Hi. I'm Isa." She displayed a huge smile, not the least bit embarrassed by her two missing front teeth.

"I'm Gavin. Come on in." He stepped aside, and she jumped over the threshold into the living room, landing with both feet planted firmly on a colorful braided area rug.

"Do you have a last name?"

"Don't you?"

"Of course." She giggled. "What's yours?"

"Powell. Why?"

"My mom says I have to call adults by their last name." She assessed him with dark brown eyes in much the same manner her mother had yesterday. "Thank you for having me here today, Mr. Powell."

Her speech sounded rehearsed, probably Sage's doing, but Gage was impressed nonetheless.

He'd once visited Cassie when she was about this age. He and Isa had already exchanged more words in two minutes than he and Cassie had during their first hour together.

In all fairness to his daughter, she hadn't been meeting an acquaintance of her mother. The man standing before her was her father, a stranger she didn't remember from his last visit three years earlier.

The horse figurine he'd brought as a gift hadn't broken the ice. How was he to know she liked Barbie dolls and dressing up? Their trip to the park had been strained, as were the next three days. How hard it must have been for Cassie to be thrust into the care of a man she barely knew and told, "This is your father."

Love wasn't something that could be manufactured on the spot just because of a biological connection.

The worst moment of that trip was when they were saying goodbye. To his astonishment, Cassie hugged him fiercely and, in a teary voice, asked him not to go. The only genuine moment they'd shared and it had to be when he was getting into the rental car and heading to the airport.

His answer, he couldn't remember it now, had just made her cry.

His next visit three years later was even more strained. And this last time, when he'd picked her up at the airport for her first-ever trip to Arizona, she'd been sullen rather than shy. Nothing much had changed in the four months since.

He must, he told himself, be patient with her. Their dysfunctionality hadn't happened overnight. It wouldn't be resolved quickly, either.

"Where's your mom?" he asked Isa.

"Right here." Sage rushed through the still-open door, pocketing her cell phone and looking completely frazzled. Her high, elegant cheekbones were flushed a vivid crimson, and several tendrils of hair hung haphazardly around her face as if pulled loose by anxious fingers. "I told you to wait for me, *mija*."

"Yes, but—" Isa's eyes widened with delight. "You have a puppy!" She dropped to her knees and opened her arms.

Cassie's puppy went right to her, drawn like iron particles to a magnet, his entire hind end shaking along with his tail.

She gathered him into her lap, giggling as he covered her chin with kisses.

"What's his name?"

"Blue."

"But he's brown and black."

"His eyes are blue."

Isa peered into the puppy's face, earning herself more kisses.

"Sorry we're late." Sage shut the door behind her. "I got tied up."

"It happens." Normally, Gavin was intolerant of tardiness. He blamed running a business with strict schedules. But something had obviously thrown Sage for a loop.

She nodded and, pushing one of the flyaway tendrils from her face, offered a pale shadow of the smile that had come so easily and naturally yesterday.

"You okay?" Gavin asked.

"Yeah. Just having a killer day."

He thought she looked more distraught and upset than overwhelmed. "Can I get you and Isa something? A soda or ice water?"

"Water would be great." She sighed as if she'd been waiting all day for just such an offer.

At that moment, Cassie poked her head into the living room. "Have you seen Blue?"

"In here. Cassie, you remember Ms. Navarre. And this is her daughter, Isa."

He'd told Cassie the reason for Sage's visit during dinner last evening and about their plans to capture the mustang. While she'd tried to act as disinterested as she did about everything that concerned him or the ranch—with the sole exception of riding and Blue—he noticed how intently she'd listened to both him and the questions Ethan posed.

Unfortunately, she was still smarting from him asking her

to leave him and Sage alone the previous day, and, as a result, talking to him only when necessary.

Okay, he'd handled the situation wrong by embarrassing her in front of company. But how was he to know? He was still at the beginning of a very long and very high learning curve. They both were. Though, as the adult in the relationship, he should be doing better.

Maybe an apology would go over better than an explanation. He'd try later. What could it hurt?

Cassie approached the little girl, and Gavin worried that she might not want someone else playing with her puppy. His concern faded when Cassie knelt down beside Isa and patted the puppy along with her.

"Hi. I'm Cassie. How old are you?"

"Six," Isa muttered under her breath, shrinking slightly.

Strange, Gavin thought. The little girl hadn't been the least bit bashful with him.

Cassie was undeterred. "I'm twelve. Do you like to ride?"

"Uh-huh."

Blue rolled onto his back, his tongue hanging out the side of his mouth, completely lost in puppy ecstasy.

"I have a horse my dad gave me. He's a registered paint."

Isa ah'd appreciatively and blurted, "Your dad said I could ride one of your horses."

"He did?" Cassie raised her gaze to Gavin.

"I thought later I'd let her give old Chico a test-drive."

"I'll take her." A spark lit Cassie's eyes, the first one Gavin had seen in a while.

For a moment, he was struck speechless. "Well…" While confident in her riding abilities, allowing her to be responsible for a six-year-old was an entirely different matter.

But there was that spark in her eyes.

"Come on, Dad. We could have an earthquake, and old Chico would just stand there."

"It's up to Isa's mom."

"Oh, please, Mommy." Isa was on her feet and throwing her arms around Sage's waist.

"I don't know. Isa has only ever ridden ponies."

"Cassie's very responsible." Were his eyes playing tricks on him? Was that actually a smile his daughter directed at him? "If it would make you feel better, we can work on the back patio. You'll be able to see the arena from there. And it's true. Chico would just stand there in an earthquake."

The lines of tension creasing Sage's brow lessened marginally. "All right," she relented after a lengthy pause.

"Can Blue come?" Isa darted back to Cassie.

"Naturally." Cassie scooped up the puppy. "He goes everywhere with me. Even sleeps with me."

The chronic pressure in Gavin's chest eased by a fraction. He was pretty certain something good had just happened between him and Cassie, but he couldn't say what exactly.

Sage stepped forward after the girls left. "We should probably get started…"

"Sorry." He tilted his head toward the kitchen. "Come on, I'll get you that water." It wasn't until they started walking that he noticed she carried a portfolio. "What did you bring?"

"Reports on a few of our recent roundup campaigns. I thought maybe we could talk a little about the techniques we're going to use."

Gavin wasn't sure what techniques the BLM used to round up large numbers of horses on federal land but doubted they'd work on a single horse roaming an urban preserve.

After retrieving his files on the mustang and filling two large plastic tumblers with ice and water, he took Sage outside. Just as he was closing the door behind them, he caught sight of his dad coming into the kitchen. He'd probably been waiting in his room for them to leave so he could start supper.

Another family member Gavin didn't relate to and didn't know what to do about. His father's depression seemed to worsen every year. Short of bringing back his mother, Gavin was out of ideas on how to cure it. Talking got nowhere, and his dad flat out refused to see a counselor, join a support group or consult with his doctor.

Ethan had no better luck than Gavin did. But then, Ethan tried less. Not that Gavin blamed him. His brother had his own problems to deal with since his discharge from the service. Their sister, Sierra, was the only one who could bring their dad out of his shell. But she lived in San Francisco and had come home only once during the past couple years. Something else that depressed their dad.

Outside, in the balmy weather, Gavin tried to put his concerns aside. It was a beautiful day, he was making plans to capture the wild mustang and Cassie wasn't mad at him anymore. At least for the moment.

It could be, and more often than not was, worse.

"THIS WAY."

Gavin escorted Sage to the large patio on the backside of the house. There, they sat at the picnic table where he and his family ate when they took their meals outside. Midafternoon sun filtered through the spindly branches of a sprawling paloverde that was easily as old as his father. Potted cacti and succulents, some of them planted by his mother, nestled along the base of the low stucco wall.

"It's very pretty here," Sage commented, glancing around before opening her portfolio and withdrawing a stack of papers. "The view's spectacular."

She was right. The McDowell Mountains and, in the far distance, Pinnacle Peak, provided a stunning backdrop.

Gavin saw the view a dozen times a day, yet he never tired of it.

He'd once felt that way about the view from the front courtyard, too, which now looked out onto the whole of Mustang Village.

"Do you think the girls are okay?" Sage peered over her shoulder toward the stables.

"If they don't come out in a few minutes, we can check on them."

"All right." She began rifling through her portfolio. A small sound of frustration escaped her lips.

Gavin waited, his doubts growing. Yesterday, she'd impressed him with her confidence, friendliness and intelligence. Today, she was like an entirely different person. Distracted, unfocused and disorganized.

What had happened to her between then and now?

"Here they are." With noticeable relief, she handed Gavin a trio of photographs. "These are from a roundup I participated in this past spring on the Navajo Nation outside of Winslow. We brought in over eighty head of horses and seven burros."

He examined the photos, two of which were aerial shots taken from the inside of what he assumed was a helicopter. The herd of horses, bunched together in a long line, resembled a rushing river as they galloped over a rocky rise and down the other side.

It must have been a majestic and thrilling sight. He could almost hear the pounding of their hooves and feel the ground shaking beneath him as they thundered past. When his great-grandfather had first settled in these parts, mustangs not unlike these had made the valley their home. To have seen these horses on the Navajo Nation would have been like witnessing a living and breathing piece of history.

He flipped to the next picture, and his heart sank low in

his chest. In this one, taken from the ground, the horses had been crowded into corrals and were milling restlessly. A few bit or kicked their neighbors. A mare tried valiantly to protect her young foal.

"It's not right, putting the horses through this." Gavin hadn't realized he'd spoken aloud until Sage answered him.

"I know it looks bad. But if we hadn't removed the horses, most of them would have died. Rainfall last winter was half of our annual average. All the area's water sources had dried up."

He studied the photo closer, noting the poor condition of the animals. Underweight, undersized and lackluster, pest-infected coats. It was fortunate the BLM had stepped in when they had. Still, removing animals from their natural environment didn't sit well with him.

"Was there no other way to help them?"

"We tried filling tanks with water. The horses were skittish and refused to drink."

Hearing the girls' animated chatter, Gavin and Sage looked up.

Cassie led Chico from the stables to the small corral beside the arena where Ethan was teaching a class of about a dozen beginner students. They trotted in a tight figure-eight pattern as their parents watched, either relaxing in lawn chairs or standing along the fence.

Isa sat astride Chico, her fists clutching the reins, her feet barely reaching the stirrups of Cassie's youth saddle. Rocking from side to side as he walked, the old horse clopped slowly along, his hips appearing more prominent because of his swayed back. Blue brought up the rear, tripping over his front paws in his attempt to keep up.

Sage watched them, her expression intent.

"Ethan learned to ride on Chico," Gavin told her.

She didn't appear to hear him.

"Isa will be fine."

He was about to repeat himself when Sage suddenly turned around and blinked as if orienting herself. Wherever she'd been the past minute was a million miles from the ranch.

"You want to postpone this?" Gavin's patience had worn thin. According to Sage, they only had a week to capture the mustang, and he resented wasting time.

"No." Picking through the papers again, she removed a typewritten report and passed it to him. "Not everyone agrees with the bureau's program of capturing feral mustangs and burros. And I won't argue with you, it's an imperfect solution. But I also believe we're doing the right thing. Saving and preserving a part of America's heritage, not destroying it." Her voice rang with unabashed passion.

It was something Gavin understood. He believed in the same thing himself.

After skimming the report, he opened his file and took out the map he used to mark the mustang's territory. Spreading it open on the table, he pointed to the *X*'s.

"These are the various places I've spotted the mustang in the last four months. You can see, he keeps to the same territory."

"Which is near the ranch."

"Within three miles, though he's come as close as half a mile. I imagine he's drawn to our horses."

She murmured her agreement. "Where does he get his water?"

Gavin was glad her attention had ceased wandering. "There could be springs, but this is desert country. I've never seen any water in the mountains except after heavy rainfall, which, as you said earlier, has been less than average of late. I'm pretty certain he drinks at the golf course." Gavin showed her the location of the country club on the map.

"You're kidding!"

"They maintain a small reservoir on the back end to feed the ponds on the course and for water in case of a fire. The maintenance people have reported all kinds of wild animals drinking there. Javelina, bobcats, coyotes and even a few deer."

Sage perked up. "Do you own any ATVs?"

"Two. Why?"

"We can use them to round up the horse."

"No, we can't. Motorized vehicles are prohibited on the preserve. And even if they weren't, they make too much noise. He'd hear us coming a mile away and take off."

"How else are we going to capture him? We have to be able to herd him in the direction we want."

"Like my grandfather and great-grandfather did. On horseback."

She shook her head. "That won't work. It'll take too long."

Her complete dismissal annoyed Gavin. "It's that or on mountain bikes."

"I hope you're joking."

"Look, Sage. I'm not the BLM. I don't have helicopters at my disposal."

"Do you know someone with a small plane?"

"Even if I did, I wouldn't enlist their help."

"I'll contact my office. Maybe they can obtain permission from the state for us to use your ATVs."

So much for her little speech about protecting and preserving America's heritage.

"Forget it. The only way we're going after this horse is the same way ranchers have for generations. With ropes and on horseback."

Their gazes connected and held fast. Hers had cooled considerably but revealed little. Gavin was certain there was no mistaking what was going through his mind.

Sage broke the silence. "How exactly are you proposing we go about it?"

"Have you ever heard of a Judas horse?"

"Yes. But I've never seen that technique put to effective use."

"There's a box canyon in the south end of the preserve. Here." Gavin tapped the map with his index finger. "We'll construct a small pen at the base of the canyon and put a couple of our mares in there. Preferably ones in heat."

"How will you construct the pen? Won't you need to haul fencing in?"

"We'll run a rope line. Use any natural materials in the area. We can pack in food and water for the mares, enough to last overnight. If all goes well, the next morning the mustang will be in the canyon with the mares. There's only one way in and out." He circled the narrow opening to the canyon.

"How many of us will there be?"

"Me, you, Ethan, Conner, he's a local cowboy who helps us out part-time, and possibly my partner." Gavin wished he could include his dad but the older man hadn't ridden in years.

Sage returned to the map. "So, we could position two riders at the entrance of the canyon, preventing the mustang's escape, and the other three could trap and rope him."

"That's the plan."

"It might work," she relented with a shrug.

"It *will* work."

"You're still counting heavily on luck."

"He'll come for the mares. I'm sure of it."

Isa's laughter reached them across the open area, once again diverting Sage's attention.

Cassie jogged alongside Chico, urging the old horse into a slow trot that delighted his rider. It pleased Gavin to see his daughter taking her responsibility seriously.

Sage's expression, however, immediately tensed.

She was, he decided, a worrywart where her daughter was concerned. He hoped that didn't cause any problems for them. The risk of danger existed with any trip into the mountains. Greater when a wild and unpredictable animal was involved. The last thing they needed was for one of them to be overly preoccupied. That was how accidents happened.

"What time do we leave tomorrow?" she asked, facing him.

"Right after breakfast. I was thinking seven. It'll be plenty light by then."

"Do you need any help getting ready?"

There was a lot of work involved. Supplies and equipment to assemble and pack. "If you're offering, I accept. But I have a four o'clock lesson and won't be ready to start until after that. Maybe you and your daughter can stay for dinner."

Gavin could use the help, it was true. But after Sage's odd behavior today, he'd grown skeptical and really wanted a chance to observe her in action. He had too much riding on capturing the mustang to take chances with a loose cannon.

"I don't want to impose," she said.

"My dad always fixes enough for an army."

Sage glanced at the girls again, her brow creasing with indecision. "I...guess so. Let me make a phone call."

"My lesson doesn't start for another twenty minutes." He refolded the map and put it back in his file. "How 'bout I meet you in the stables after you make your call."

"Fine." Sage also collected her materials.

As they stood, a pickup truck rolled through the open area in front of the stables at a speed slightly faster than Gavin would have preferred. Rather than pull behind the stables and park in the area reserved for visitors, the driver came to a dust-billowing stop in front of the hitching rail.

If it were anyone else, Gavin would have a stern word with them. In this case, he simply ground his teeth.

Dan Rivera didn't think rules—*any* rules, not just those at Powell Ranch—applied to him. It came from having a very elevated opinion of himself and his abilities. On the other hand, he *was* a good horse trainer and brought several new customers to the ranch. He was also an astute businessman and had helped Gavin immensely.

So, though it annoyed him, he let the speeding and parking violations slide.

Sage had taken out her cell phone and was punching in numbers. When she caught sight of Dan emerging from his truck, she stopped cold and swore under her breath.

"Do you know him?" Gavin asked.

"Unfortunately, yes." Her hands shaking, she pocketed her cell without completing the call.

Dan headed in the direction of the parents at the fence, several of whom were his clients.

Sage's eyes widened with fright as she tracked his every step. "I need to get my daughter." She started out at a brisk walk.

"What's wrong?" Gavin lengthened his strides to catch up.

"I'm sorry," she stuttered. "We can't stay for dinner after all."

With that, she broke into a fast run.

SAGE'S HEART BEAT WITH such force she thought it might shatter. Her ex was on a collision course with Isa, and unless Sage sprouted wings, she wasn't going to get there ahead of him.

Dammit! She didn't want her daughter meeting her father for the first time in four years with no preparation.

Her fault. All her fault. She'd known Gavin had dealings

with Dan. She should have at least anticipated the possibility of running into him at the ranch.

"Sage!" Gavin appeared alongside her just as Dan was approaching Isa.

Suddenly, as if a button had been pushed, everything slowed to a crawl and each detail crystalized into sharp focus. Sage watched, horrified and helpless, as Isa trotted along the corral fence within a few feet of Dan. He stared ahead at the parents watching Ethan's class. Then all at once, Sage's worst fears were realized. Dan turned his head and looked directly at Isa.

Oh, God! Please don't let him say something hurtful.

Sage stumbled to a stop. She tried to breathe but her fire-filled lungs wouldn't expand.

The moment—which seemed to last an eternity—abruptly passed.

Dan continued walking without so much as breaking a single step.

He hadn't recognized his own daughter!

"You bastard!" Sage's previously stalled breath came in ragged bursts.

"What the hell's going on?"

She'd forgotten about Gavin. "Nothing."

"That wasn't nothing."

Sit. She needed to sit before her knees gave out. "It's personal."

"If you have issues with Dan Rivera, I want to know."

Sage had to get out of sight. Immediately. Dan may not have recognized Isa, but if he saw her, he'd put two and two together.

She spun on her heels and hurried to the stables, praying Dan wouldn't decide to go in there.

Gavin was right behind her. The moment they were inside, he reached for her arm.

"Sage."

"Can you go ask Cassie to bring Isa here?"

"Not until you tell me—"

"It's none of your business."

His intense blue eyes drilled into her. Held her in place. "If this involves Dan, it most certainly is my business."

"Why?" she snapped. "Because he's the local horse trainer?"

"Because he's my partner in the stud and breeding business. The one I'm starting with the mustang. And he's also my financial backing."

Shaken to her core, she retreated a step. "No, no, no. We're not working together." She shook her head vehemently. "The deal's off."

"The hell it is." His voice rose. "You agreed."

Her reply was cut short by Cassie leading the old horse into the stables, Isa still sitting astride him. Both the girls' faces registered alarm.

"Dad? What's going on?"

Chapter Four

Sage was still shaking. She only half heard the exchange between Gavin and his daughter, too caught up in her own whirling emotions.

"Everything's fine," he answered Cassie's question with admirable calm.

"It didn't look fine." She faced him, her puppy tucked beneath one arm, the old horse's reins wrapped in the fingers of her free hand. "It looked like you were arguing."

"We were just talking."

"Yeah." Cassie's narrowed gaze pinged between Sage and her father.

Fortunately, Isa was oblivious to everyone and everything around her save the horse.

"Chico, you're such a good boy." She leaned forward over the saddle horn and gave the horse's neck an affectionate squeeze. He lived up to his reputation by bearing the attention with gentlemanly grace. "Did you see me riding, Mama?"

"I did, *mija*." Sage went over and placed a hand on Isa's knee. "You were awesome."

The minute Dan paid the back child support—and he would, she'd see to it—she was going to buy Isa that pony. She should have purchased one sooner, but the cost of keeping and feeding a second horse was more than she could comfortably afford on her income.

Damn Dan again for denying Isa the money that was rightfully hers. And damn him for putting both her and Sage through the ordeal of a paternity test—though she suspected it was just another postponement ploy.

Last evening, her cousin and Roberto had tried convincing her that a positive paternity test would only strengthen her case against Dan. They were right, of course. The knowledge, however, didn't lessen her angst.

"Are you sure?" Cassie demanded, returning Sage to the present.

"Ms. Navarre and I were just discussing the best method to go after the mustang."

"Loudly."

Sage bit back a groan. Gavin talked to his daughter as if she was Isa's age. Did he not see how astute Cassie was and that very little got past her?

The sound of distant voices reminded Sage of her and Isa's precarious situation. She had to remove them from sight before Dan noticed them. She began looking for another way out of the stables.

"You okay, Mama?"

"Just a little tired." She sent Isa a reassuring smile. In truth, Sage was perspiring profusely, probably from the giant invisible fist squeezing her insides.

She still couldn't believe Dan had failed to recognize his own daughter. Granted, children changed a lot between two and six. But even so...

"If it's none of my business," Cassie grumbled, "say so."

Gavin quirked an eyebrow. "If I do, will you get mad?"

"Honestly, Dad." She expelled an irritated sigh.

Sage didn't blame her. She'd tried reasoning with Gavin, too, and it had gotten her nowhere. How he managed not to chase away every customer on the place with his confounding obstinance was a mystery.

"Fine." Cassie deposited Blue on the ground by her feet. He immediately stumbled over to Gavin and launched an assault on his boot, gnawing the rounded toe. Gavin bent and scratched the puppy behind the ears.

Interesting, thought Sage. He was tolerant of small, defenseless dogs, passionate about the plight of wild horses and hadn't mentioned her meltdown to his daughter.

Which meant he wasn't all bad.

Figures.

If only he weren't in partnership with her ex.

That was one shortcoming Sage couldn't overlook or dismiss regardless of how good-looking she found him.

Fresh thoughts of Dan squashed whatever fleeting and irrational attraction she felt toward Gavin. Her glance strayed yet again to the stable entrance, and her ears strained for the sound of his truck starting up and leaving.

No such luck.

Sage began to fidget, her mind searching for an excuse to leave—if not the ranch, then at least the immediate vicinity.

Gavin beat her to the punch. "Cassie, why don't you take Isa inside for a little while?"

"What about Chico?"

"I'll unsaddle him and put him away."

She frowned. "You told me if I rode a horse, it was my responsibility to walk him out, brush him down and put him away."

"We'll make an exception today."

"This is pure bull—"

"Cassie." His expression grew dark.

"—droppings," she finished with a glare.

He took the reins from her and turned to Isa. "You ready to get off, young lady?"

"Do I have to?" Her bottom lip protruded in a disappointed pout.

"'Fraid so." Sage lifted Isa from the saddle, relief surging through her.

"Tell you what." Gavin patted the little girl's head once she was standing. "You can ride Chico again the next time your mom brings you out."

"Really?"

"As much as you want."

"Tomorrow?"

He laughed. "Okay by me, but you'll have to wait until we get back from our trip into the mountains."

"Can I, Mama? Please?" Isa clasped her small hands in front of her.

"We'll see."

Sage was doubting the wisdom of bringing Isa back to Powell Ranch ever again. Not with Dan coming and going like he did. "Tia Anna and Tio Roberto were going to watch you. Take you to the movies." She put a hand on Isa's shoulder and nudged her along. "Come on, I'll go with you and Cassie. We both need to wash up."

Was there a less conspicuous route to the house? She'd ask Cassie the second they were away from Gavin.

Before she took so much as a step, he said, "Stay. We can finish our...talk."

Not exactly an order, but more than a request.

Sage's stomach sank. She should have expected this— Gavin wasn't a man easily put off. And any objections she made would only further delay the girls leaving.

Choosing the lesser of two evils, she murmured, "All right, I'll stay," and sent Isa off with Cassie, praying Dan was too preoccupied with his clients to glance in their direction.

"SORRY ABOUT THAT," GAVIN told Sage once they were alone. "She doesn't generally use bad language. Or if she does," he added wryly, "it's not around me."

Sage fought the need to pace. Gavin's problems with his daughter didn't concern her. She had enough of her own to worry about. "Isa's been around livestock enough to have heard the word *droppings*."

How long would it take the girls to reach the house? Three minutes? Five?

"I should probably have another talk with my brother. He's the bad influence on Cassie. Too many years in the Marines."

Gavin led Chico over to the hitching rail and slung the reins over it. The old horse just stood there. If he did realize he wasn't tied, he didn't care. Gavin unbuckled the girth and let it drop. Chico heaved a tired sigh, and his eyes drooped closed.

"I'm also sorry I raised my voice earlier." Gavin pulled the small youth saddle off Chico's back and held it in one hand by the horn. "When you said you weren't going with us to capture the mustang, I lost my temper." He removed the saddle blanket next. "But you gave as good as you got."

She didn't disagree.

"Cassie and I are still working out the kinks in our relationship," he said after returning from the tack room, minus the saddle and blanket.

"My mother frequently reminds me that's why children were put on this earth."

Sage was tired of discussing Isa and Cassie. They weren't the reason Gavin had detained her. Trying not to be obvious, she peered over her shoulder. No sight of Dan or Isa. Still, she couldn't relax.

When she turned back around, it was to discover Gavin staring at her.

"What exactly went on back there?" he asked. "I take it you know Dan Rivera."

Sage thought fast. If she told Gavin about Dan, he might

understand and not insist they work together. One glance at the determined set of his square jaw promptly squashed that idea. He could possibly refuse to help her capture the mustang. After specifically requesting this assignment from her supervisor, she couldn't return to Show Low with an empty trailer.

Though it galled her, she was going to have to level with Gavin. At least a little.

"Dan Rivera is Isa's father."

"Wow." He pushed his cowboy hat back and rubbed his forehead. "Not the answer I was expecting."

"He hasn't seen Isa in four years or had any contact with her whatsoever."

Gavin nodded as if he understood, only he couldn't possibly.

"I didn't want him talking to Isa without me…preparing her first."

"Did you know he was here?"

"I knew he lived in Mustang Village. But not that he was your partner or that he'd be here today."

Gavin removed a halter from a peg on the wall and swapped it out for Chico's bridle.

"I realize Dan being my partner is awkward for you," he said.

"More than awkward."

"But I don't see how it makes a difference."

She stared at him over the horse's neck. "I just told you he's my ex. My *estranged* ex."

Gavin began brushing Chico. "Look. We capture the mustang this weekend like we planned. Afterward, during the rest of your stay, Dan and I work with the mustang while you and he decide whatever it is you need to about Isa. Then, when you leave, he and I go back to business as usual."

Sage was certain it wouldn't be that simple. In fact, she

could guarantee it. First thing Monday she was contacting the Child Support Enforcement Agency and having garnishment papers sent here. If the Powells owed Dan any fees or commissions, she'd be able to attach them. A move like that would surely put a strain on Dan and Gavin's partnership.

If all went well and the DES moved at their usual speed, she'd be long gone by the time the papers arrived.

Something Gavin mentioned earlier came rushing back to her. "Did you say that Dan was going with us to capture the mustang?"

"Yeah."

"Well, he can't. Not if you want me along."

Gavin considered that for several seconds. "Are you going to sic the authorities on me for capturing the mustang on my own?"

Sage regretted having made such a big deal about the law. "There has to be another solution."

"How about you and Dan put your personal differences aside for one weekend?" Gavin ran the brush over the old horse's rump and down his back legs.

Could they? It wasn't as though Isa would be going with them on their trek into the mountains. "Even if I agree," she said, "I'm not sure Dan will."

Not after yesterday. He'd probably expect her to serve him with the child support orders again.

"Do you want to talk to him or should I?"

As much as Sage wished she could refuse accompanying Gavin on the mustang roundup, she had a responsibility. She'd also given Gavin her word.

A low groan involuntarily escaped her. How had she wound up in this predicament?

Gavin set the brush on the hitching rail. "Maybe we both should talk to him."

Sage shook her head, mortified at the prospect. "I don't think so."

When she'd phoned Dan this morning to tell him the DNA testing facility she'd contacted required a sample from him along with Isa, he'd hung up on her. Yesterday, he'd slammed the door in her face. No guarantee what he'd do if she approached him with Gavin in tow, requesting he put their personal differences aside.

"You sure?" Gavin asked. "Because he's coming this way."

"What? No!"

Sage whirled around and panicked at the sight of Dan strolling up the aisle with a woman and a teenage boy about Cassie's age.

"I have to leave." Even as Sage recognized how cowardly she sounded, she started off in the opposite direction of Dan. She refused to deal with him. Not until the paternity test was done and not in front of people.

People being Gavin Powell.

This wasn't like her. She didn't run away from problems, she faced them. But Dan's cold treatment of her and unreasonable demands had really shaken her. Sage long ago admitted her part in their breakup. She was hardly a perfect person. But infidelity wasn't and never had been one of her faults. That he should imply as much outraged her. It also hurt.

"Wait." Gavin drew up beside her, Chico trotting to keep pace.

She didn't slow down.

"Sage, he's not following us."

She dared a backward glance. Dan and his companions had stopped in front of a stall, observing the occupant and conversing. She doubted he'd spotted her. Still, she took no chances and continued hurrying.

Gavin reached over and, placing a hand on her shoulder, maneuvered her in front of him. "He won't see you this way."

Assistance was the last thing she'd expected from him. Not when two minutes ago he'd been insisting she speak to Dan.

"Which way to the house?" she asked when they emerged on the other end of the stables.

"We're not going to the house. Not yet."

"You may not be, but I am."

"Come on."

Before she could object, he took her hand and guided her toward a fenced pasture with several noticeably pregnant mares.

Sage might be distraught but she couldn't help noticing the confident ease with which his fingers held hers. Firm, yet gentle and not entirely unpleasant. Neither was the sensation of walking beside him. Men with his height and brawn could be intimidating and overbearing. If anything, the response Gavin's nearness evoked in her was that of being sheltered and protected.

She'd all but forgotten what it felt like.

His stoic expression gave no clue to what was going through his mind or if being close to her was similarly affecting him.

"Where are you taking me?" she asked in an effort to steer her thoughts in a different—and safer—direction.

"First, we're putting old Chico away. He won't mind spending a night with the girls. Then, we're heading inside for dinner. Later, you can help me and Ethan pack for tomorrow. Cassie will watch Isa."

Just as they'd agreed to earlier. Before Dan had driven onto the ranch. Except now she wasn't so inclined to go along.

"And at some point," he continued, "when we find a few minutes alone, you're going to tell me exactly what's going on with you and Dan."

"I don't think so." Sage came to a grinding halt. The abrupt movement separated Gavin's hand from hers.

She told herself she didn't miss his touch.

He opened the gate to the pasture, and the old horse dutifully meandered through it, far more interested in what the feed trough might hold than the mares.

"Look, Sage." Gavin shut and latched the gate. "I'm going to capture the wild horse. I need your cooperation and you need mine to get your job done. Dan's my business associate and partner. I'm pretty sure I can convince him to work with you. But I need to know what's going on. I'm not asking for your life story or all the gritty details. The *Reader's Digest* version will do fine."

His blue eyes assessed her closely. It surprised her to see compassion and sympathy in their arresting depths. Not judgment.

Slowly, she relented.

"Okay. Isa and I will stay for dinner, and I'll help you and Ethan pack." She told herself she owed him that much for helping her evade Dan.

How much of her guts she would spill during their "few minutes alone," however, remained to be seen.

Hand-holding aside, Gavin was still Dan's partner, and she didn't trust him.

Chapter Five

Gavin tried to remember the last time a woman had shared dinner with his family. With the exception of his sister, Sierra, whose previous visit had been almost two years ago, it was...

No one. Not after his mother died and neighbors and friends stopped coming around.

The Powell men, he noticed, were all having different reactions to Sage and her young daughter, including himself. Ethan had assumed the role of host, asking Sage questions about her job and living in Show Low. Gavin's father was polite, though guarded, having not yet decided how big a threat these intruders were to his orderly world.

Sage had definitely threatened Gavin's orderly world, but for entirely different reasons. She was a mystery, exasperating one moment and fascinating the next. It had been a lot of years since he'd felt the sweet tug of attraction. That the woman should be Sage, an unsuitable choice for many reasons, confounded him—and intrigued him.

Once inside the safety of the house, she still hadn't relaxed. Not until Dan's pickup rolled out of the ranch some twenty minutes later. Whatever he'd done to her and Isa must have been very hurtful for Sage to have reacted like she had. Especially after four years.

His common sense warned him to steer clear of her. That she had emotional baggage. More than just carry-on.

But then there was that sweet tug.

"How long have you worked for the BLM?" Ethan asked, and proceeded to shovel an impressive bite of spaghetti into his mouth.

"Eight years." Unlike Ethan, Sage picked at her meal, consuming only half of what she pushed around on her plate.

"What made you decide to work for them?"

"A friend actually convinced me to apply."

"Did she also work for the BLM?"

"Um, he did, yes."

It was less that the friend was a man than the hesitancy in Sage's voice that roused Gavin's curiosity. He'd like to hear the parts of the story she was omitting.

Ethan continued chatting amiably with their guests. He'd always been the more outgoing one, with Gavin preferring to listen rather than talk. Ethan was equally willing to talk about himself and considered himself an open book. Except when it came to his leg. That was a topic he didn't discuss, even with his family.

"Have you always had horses?"

"Actually, no. Not until community college when I took a riding class because I thought it would be an easy A." Sage gave a small laugh. "Turns out, it wasn't so easy. But I loved the class and now horses aren't just my job, they're my life."

"My papa's a horse trainer."

At Isa's announcement, Sage's fork clattered to her plate. Sending an embarrassed glance around the table, she picked it up.

"Really?" Ethan winked at Isa then went for seconds of the tossed salad. "That's neat."

"What kind of horse trainer?" Cassie asked.

She and Isa had become fast buddies, which was more than

Gavin could say about any of the kids at school. Principal Rodgers had told him Cassie didn't relate well to her peers. She related well to younger children, as evidenced by her busy babysitting schedule, and had taken Isa under her wing from the moment they met.

"I don't know." Isa looked questioningly at Sage.

"Western equestrian mostly," she replied.

"He lives in Mustang Village," Isa added with a bright, lop-sided smile. "That's why we came here. So I can see him."

"The only horse trainer I know of in Mustang Village is—"

Gavin shook his head but his brother didn't notice.

"—Dan Rivera."

"That's him." Isa jiggled gleefully in her seat.

Sage paled.

"No fooling?" Ethan grinned. "He was just here—"

"The other day," Gavin cut in.

"No, he—"

"Yes, the other day," he repeated, and shook his head again.

This time, Ethan saw him and shut up.

"Cassie, why don't you and Isa help me serve the dessert?" Gavin's father suggested, rising from the table. "We have chocolate pudding."

Both girls jumped up to help.

If Gavin didn't know better, he might have thought his father was intentionally diverting a disaster.

The remainder of dinner passed without incident, though the quizzical stare Ethan aimed at Gavin was hard to ignore. When they were done, their father recruited the girls' assistance again, this time to clear the table and load the dishwasher.

"Do you mind keeping an eye on Isa while her mom, Uncle Ethan and I pack for tomorrow?"

To Gavin's relief, Cassie was agreeable.

"Come on, pip-squeak." She didn't have to ask twice. Isa was hot on her heels in a heartbeat, and the two of them began carting dishes to the sink.

Sage remained subdued as she, Gavin and Ethan walked to the stables. It had grown dark during dinner but their path was illuminated by two exterior lights, one on the back porch and the other mounted above the entrance to the stables. Inside, Gavin flipped a switch and more lights came on, startling some of the horses that weren't used to so much activity after dark.

Gavin extracted a handwritten list from his pocket as they approached the tack room. "I was thinking two packhorses should be enough."

While he and Ethan collected and debated over the various equipment and supplies they would be taking, Sage carried three large canteens to the water spigot outside and filled them. She had only just returned when Ethan's cell phone rang.

He answered it and after a brief, cryptic conversation ended with "See you in half an hour."

"Going somewhere?" Gavin asked.

"Is it a problem? I can stay if you need me to."

"No, it's all right. There isn't much left." If not for wanting to get Sage alone so they could finish their earlier conversation, Gavin might have waylaid his brother and pumped him for more information. This was the third time in the past two weeks he'd left after receiving a phone call and without saying exactly where he was going.

They hurried through the remainder of the packing. "Come on and walk with me," Gavin said the moment Ethan was gone.

"Where?"

"I need help carrying the feed for the mares we're leaving

in the canyon overnight." He didn't hurry in the hopes she'd take a cue from him and relax. She didn't. He decided to try a different tactic.

"Cassie's only been living with me since the summer. Before that, she was with her mother full-time. In Connecticut."

"That's quite a ways from Arizona."

They reached the barrels in the hay shed behind the stables where the grain and pellets were stored.

"Her mom moved to Manchester not long after Cassie was born. I only got to see her about every three years. Not by choice. I was young when she was born. Barely twenty-one. My mother had just passed away after a long illness. Money was scarce. We'd sold off most of the ranch two years earlier along with our cattle operation. I didn't have a job, and the only thing I knew how to do was raise cattle."

"Why are you telling me this?"

"You mentioned that Dan hasn't seen Isa in four years. I just thought it might help if you—"

"Dan didn't want to see Isa. And trust me, he's had plenty of chances. He may not want to see her now, which will really disappoint her. You saw at dinner how excited she is."

Gavin had seen. And he had to admit, he didn't understand his partner. He'd have given his right arm to be a bigger part of Cassie's life during her childhood. Maybe then they'd have the kind of close relationship he yearned for.

Setting down the scoop he'd been using to fill the sack with pellets, he removed his cell phone from his belt and dialed a number. When a familiar female voice answered, he said, "Hi, Maria, is Dan there?"

"What are you doing?" Sage hissed.

Gavin angled the phone away from his mouth. "We're leaving in the morning at 7 a.m. sharp. The problem or issue or whatever's going on with you and Dan has got to be resolved by then. There's too much riding on capturing the mustang for it not to be."

"More than you know."

Gavin pressed the disconnect button on his phone. "Tell me."

She remained stubbornly quiet.

"How can I help with Dan if you don't level with me."

"I don't see how you can help."

"He's an intelligent man whose priority is to make money. He'll do what's right for our partnership."

"Dan doesn't give a rat's hind end about anyone but himself."

Gavin didn't agree with Sage. He'd seen Dan go above and beyond for his wife, son, friends and clients. But Sage's anger at him was clearly real and deep and, in her mind at least, justified.

"I admit, he's egotistical. But he's basically a decent guy."

"Yeah. Well how many decent guys do you know who refuse to pay their court-ordered child support and haven't for almost four years?"

Her outburst stunned Gavin into silence. Dan didn't strike him as someone who turned his back on fiscal and moral obligations. If anything, it was the opposite. Which was why Gavin trusted Dan enough to become his partner.

"I'm...sorry, Sage." What else could he say? "I can understand why you didn't want him to see Isa today."

"It's complicated," she replied meekly.

"I'm sure it is."

"I don't understand him."

Neither did Gavin. He may not have visited Cassie as often as he'd wanted to, but he'd never failed to send so much as one child support payment or even been late, regardless of how strapped the family had been for money.

"I'm pretty sure I can convince him not to come with us tomorrow."

"You said before he's your partner and financial backing and entitled to go."

"He is. And the extra man would come in handy."

"Then why take the chance?"

"Because four of us working well together will be better than five, two of whom are at odds."

"I can handle Dan without your interference."

"Is that so?" Gavin scratched his chin thoughtfully. "Because earlier today you had no problem with me interfering."

"Dan caught me off guard," she defended herself. "Tomorrow, I'll be ready."

She put up a brave front. Her eyes gave her away. She wasn't ready to face Dan and less ready to work with him. Gavin couldn't risk their expedition into the mountains going awry.

Taking out his phone again, he punched Dan's number. This time, Dan answered rather than his wife. Gavin skipped any customary preambles. "I don't know if you're aware of this or not, but the BLM agent who arrived yesterday, the one who will be going with us to capture the mustang, is someone you know. Sage Navarre."

Gavin tried not to read anything into the lengthy pause that followed. Beside him, Sage rubbed her palms nervously along the sides of her jeans.

He began to doubt the wisdom of his plan.

Not that he and Cassie's mother got along famously. A part of him still resented her for the pressure she and her parents had skillfully applied on him during the vulnerable time in his life after his mother died. But when they did speak, he was always civil and agreeable for Cassie's sake *and* his own.

He didn't want to give her mother any reason to deny him visitation or turn his daughter against him.

"Do you really need me to go with you?" Dan asked, his tone revealing nothing.

"We can manage with four of us." That was their original plan anyway before Sage arrived.

"Then I'll stay home and go with you next time."

"If all goes well, we won't need a next time." He and Sage exchanged glances. Hers was hopeful.

"Good luck," Dan said, and hung up after a quick goodbye. Not at all like him. He usually talked Gavin's ear off.

"He's not coming."

Sage's shoulders sagged. "Thank you."

"No problem."

She smiled, the first honest one she'd given him since they met.

The radiance from it went straight to his heart where it warmed the dark corners left cold for so long.

In that moment Gavin knew he was a man in serious trouble.

SAGE STOOD TO THE SIDE, pulling her jacket snug against the early morning chill. She'd like to be more help, and had offered repeatedly, but the fact was she'd probably be a hindrance. Gavin, Ethan and Conner, their cowboy friend, were a well-oiled machine. They saddled up the horses, hefted the panniers onto the pack saddles, then loaded the supplies, equipment and feed. Their efficiency let Sage know this was hardly their first expedition into the mountains.

Ethan's next remark confirmed it. "Remember that time Dad took our Boy Scout troop on a pack trip to Pinnacle Peak?"

"I'm still mad about that," Conner joked, loading a five-gallon jug of water. "You guys left me and Gary Cohen at the bottom of that ravine for five hours. Without food or water. We thought we were goners."

"Not our fault you went looking for a shortcut."

"Your dad told us to. Said if we were going to keep bellyaching, we could just figure out a way home on our own. What kind of Boy Scout leader does that?" Conner shook his head, but there was laughter in his voice.

"He didn't think you'd really take off."

"Gary used our only match to set our shirts on fire and signal for help with the smoke."

"And it worked." Ethan clapped Conner affectionately on the back as he walked past. "We found you."

Sage was certain Conner and his friend were never in any real danger and had more fun than he was letting on.

"I didn't talk to your dad for a whole year. Which was pretty hard considering he was also our baseball coach."

Chuckling, Gavin covered the bulging panniers with a large plastic tarp. He and Ethan had decided on three packhorses in total, two of them mares they intended on leaving overnight. The heavy tarps covering the panniers would protect the feed, equipment and supplies from damage or falling out along the trail, which had been described to Sage as challenging.

"It's a miracle any of us survived to grow up," Conner said good-naturedly. "If your dad wasn't trying to kill us on the trail, he was working us to death on the baseball field."

"Those were the days." Ethan's smile was wistful and, Sage noted, a little sad.

So was Gavin's.

"It was a shame about your mom," Conner confessed, securing a galvanized steel tub to the top of the pack saddle frame with a piece of twine. "Don't think your dad's ever gotten over her."

Neither brother commented.

After a moment, Gavin glanced around. "We should get a move on. It's plenty light now. You ready, Sage?"

"Yeah." She nodded, curious about Gavin's mother but not wanting to ask. The man they'd been describing in their stories didn't at all resemble the quiet and subdued one she'd met at dinner the previous night.

"Mount up!"

Sage noticed that Ethan climbed onto his big bay gelding from the right side rather than the left, as was usual. She promptly forgot about it when Avaro began acting up.

"Quiet, girl," she soothed. After not being ridden for three full days, one of those spent cooped up in a trailer, the young horse was, as the saying went, feeling her oats.

Sage, not so much. Despite Gavin's conviction that they would capture the mustang, she remained dubious. In all her time at the BLM, she'd never seen a single horse willingly submit to capture. Gavin's mustang would be no different.

There was considerable shifting, prancing, nipping and scuffling until order was established and the packhorses grew accustomed to their loads. Drawing stares from the few regulars out this early on a Saturday morning, they rode through the ranch and out a gate behind the empty cattle barn.

Avaro refused to settle down and tested Sage's patience. The mare's behavior worsened as they rode along the pasture where the Powell broodmares and their young trotted along beside the fence.

At the far end of the pasture, Ethan turned his horse onto a dirt road that bore the imprint of hundreds of horse hooves. Within minutes, they were in the foothills. Soon after that, the road narrowed to a trail that rose upward at a steep angle. They automatically formed a single-file line, the horses walking nose to tail.

Sage chose to bring up the rear, not sure how Avaro would act with another horse so close behind her and in unfamiliar surroundings. Her worries proved unfounded. Avaro attacked the steep trail with the same enthusiasm she did everything else, instinctively following the pack mare behind Gavin.

At a fork in the trail, they took the higher, more rugged branch. Very soon, all the horses were noticeably laboring. Stopping atop a rise, they let their mounts rest. During their ascent, Sage had been intent on the trail and watching where Avaro placed her feet. Looking around, she gave a small surprised gasp.

The view was nothing less than spectacular.

Behind them lay the ranch and Mustang Village, nestled in the heart of the valley. Ahead of them stretched the mountains, a series of peaks and gullies that went on as far as the eye could see. To their right was the city of Scottsdale and beyond that, Phoenix. The metropolitan area stretched for miles and miles, bordered on all sides by deep brown and vibrant green mountains not unlike the one they were on. A dazzling blue sky hung overhead.

"I'd love to see this at night with all the city lights."

"I'll bring you if you want," Gavin said.

Sage's remark had been offhand, but he'd taken it seriously. "I probably won't have time while I'm here."

He shrugged and turned to face forward in his saddle.

Had her easy dismissal of his invitation hurt him? She told herself no, that Gavin wasn't a sensitive man. But guilt ate at her nonetheless. He'd only been trying to be nice.

"How much farther?" she asked when Gavin and Ethan were finished discussing the condition of the trail, which had deteriorated since the summer monsoons.

"About another hour." Gavin pointed. "See that butte over there? The box canyon is on the other side."

It looked far away. Really far. And the going a little treacherous. Okay, a lot. Sage figured she'd better have some water while she could and unwound her canteen from where it hung on her saddle horn.

Avaro began pawing the ground.

"Let's see if you're still raring to go when we reach the top of the next rise," she muttered, and rehung her canteen.

Conversation was at a minimum during the rest of the ride. Partly because they were so spread out and partly because of the noise generated from seven horses' hooves hitting the hard, rocky ground simultaneously.

Sage spotted wildlife everywhere she looked. Hawks, rabbits, coyotes, lizards and even a king snake. Any larger animals, including the mustang, surely heard them coming from a mile away and were long gone. Except for javelina.

"Look over there," Gavin said.

At the bottom of a ravine, a small herd of about eight or nine of the wild pigs scuttled through the brush.

Dropping his reins, Ethan cupped his hands around his mouth and made an odd grunting sound. The two largest javelina stopped, the row of inky bristles on their back standing straight up.

"Boars," Gavin told her.

"Do you hunt them?" she asked.

"Not since I was a kid. My grandfather used to take Ethan and me. We lost interest in high school."

"Sports?"

"That and rodeoing."

"What were your events?"

"Everything. But I was best at roping and steer wrestling."

"Did Ethan rodeo, too?"

"He was one of the top junior bull and bronc riders in the state."

"Did he compete professionally?"

"No." Gavin shook his head. Before Sage could ask why,

he told her. "My mother got sick. After she died, Ethan joined the Marines and I took over running the ranch."

His expression shut down, letting Sage know the subject was closed.

"Come on," Ethan called over his shoulder, and urged his horse ahead.

The rest of them followed without any encouragement.

Sage didn't know the Powells well, but after spending three days in their company, she'd reached the conclusion that whatever happened to Gavin's mother had profoundly affected the entire family—in ways they were still grappling with even today.

Chapter Six

One well-placed step at a time, the horses descended what had to be the steepest trail so far. Sage leaned back in the saddle, instinctively balancing her weight.

At the bottom, the riders continued to the entrance of the box canyon, the walls of which rose five stories high. Progress was slow, hampered by a particularly rugged patch of ground.

"Not much farther," Gavin announced.

Sage refrained from crying out with joy. She considered herself a competent horsewoman and spent many hours a week on Avaro. None of those hours were a tenth as grueling as this morning's ride had been. The constant up and down had strained her back and legs and knees especially. Fifteen minutes ago she'd developed an aggravating stitch in her side.

To her annoyance, Gavin, Ethan and Conner didn't appear any worse for the wear. Then again, they'd grown up in these mountains and probably took ranch customers on trail rides like this one all the time. Customers who surely fared worse than her.

That didn't stop her from hiding her aches and pains and utter exhaustion.

"How's this spot?" Ethan asked when they reached the tapered end of the canyon.

Gavin's answer was to dismount.

Sage did, too, only her legs betrayed her by buckling. Clinging to her saddle horn, she waited until the worst of the tremors subsided.

"You okay?" He appeared beside her.

Great. Just what she needed. An audience. "Fine," she answered with false enthusiasm.

To her surprise, she wasn't the only one suffering. Ethan limped in a wobbly circle, favoring his left leg, then bent to massage his knee.

She tried not to think of the ride back later or that they would be doing this all over again tomorrow. If only they'd brought the ATVs like she wanted.

Then again, they might have missed seeing all the wonderful scenery on ATVs. They *definitely* would have missed seeing the wildlife.

"You mind giving me a hand with this?" Gavin hadn't needed to cling to his saddle horn or walk off his pain. He'd immediately started unloading the pack saddles.

"What do you need me to do?"

"Stand on the other side."

She tethered Avaro to a creosote bush. Not her first choice, but it was that or a saguaro cactus. Though not quite as worn as Sage, every ounce of spunk had been ridden out of the young horse. Sage patted her rump. "Told you so."

She was no sooner in position on the other side of the pack mare than Gavin started untying the rope. He alternately threw it over the top of the pack saddle for her to catch or passed it beneath the horse for her to grab. It was like opening an intricately wrapped Christmas present. Ethan and Conner were going through an identical process with the other packhorse, only a little faster. They'd already moved onto the gelding by the time Sage and Gavin finished.

He could have complained about being stuck with the slow-poke, except he didn't.

"I thought from looking at the map the canyon would be bigger." Her gaze wandered as they folded the tarp into a compact square.

"I'm glad it's not. The small size is what makes it ideal for capturing wild horses. Less work."

Sage imagined rounding up an entire herd like Gavin's grandfather had done and driving them into the box canyon. Then she thought about driving the horses back to the ranch and how much work it must have been. Probably required a dozen men and a full week.

Thank goodness they had only one horse to worry about.

"What if the mustang's gone to the other side of the mountain range?" The McDowell Mountains stretched for at least twenty miles in a practically straight line running north and south.

"This is his territory," Gavin said. "He hasn't ventured from it the entire time I've been tracking him."

Sage didn't share Gavin's confidence. She knew feral horses, and they frequently established new territories when intruders appeared—which was exactly how the mustang would see strange people and horses.

She hated thinking they were going through all this effort for nothing.

They made quick work of unloading. Before long, piles of equipment and supplies were laid out on the ground.

"We'll leave the pack saddles and panniers overnight," Gavin said, unfurling the nylon line they would use for their makeshift pen. "Stack them over there by that boulder."

The panniers were heavy, even empty. When Sage was done, she went in search of rocks and anything else that might come in handy.

After some debate, Gavin and Ethan selected a natural shelter along the canyon wall for the location of the pen. Though the ground was uneven, the overhang would provide adequate shade.

Sage studied the shelter as she carried rocks to it. Would the mares be safe? She wouldn't want to leave Avaro in the wild overnight.

"What about predators?" she asked Gavin. "Any risk?"

"Not likely."

"But not impossible?"

"Quit worrying, Sage."

He hefted a rock at least twice the size of the ones she'd found and lugged it over to the pile. Ethan laid out the pen, marking the four corners with some of the rocks while Conner untied a bundle of metal fence posts.

Sage paused to watch. There was something about men at work that struck a chord in her—reminding her that they were bigger, stronger, more physically capable than women. It was also...sexy.

Gavin was sexy.

The sound of Ethan driving fence posts into the ground with a rubber mallet drew her attention away from his brother. As soon as he was finished with one post, he started on the next. Sage carried more rocks to the pen, ignoring the nagging twinge in her back.

This will pass, she thought, *with a hot bath and a couple of aspirins.*

All at once, Ethan lost his balance and went down on his knees, the rubber mallet flying from his hands. He let out a deep "Oomph" as he pitched forward onto all fours.

Sage dropped her rock and started toward him. "Ethan! You okay?"

Gavin was instantly beside her, his hand on her arm restraining her. "Leave him alone," he said in a soft voice.

Ethan was already picking himself up and dusting himself off.

"He could be hurt," she protested.

"He won't want your help. Or mine, for that matter."

"Are you crazy?" She noticed Conner hadn't moved, either. What was wrong with them? They all three were taking this macho guy thing way too far.

Gavin bent and retrieved her rock. "It's important for Ethan that he do things on his own."

"Come on, Gavin. Enough already. It's not like he's disabled."

"Not disabled." He placed the rock in Sage's hands. "But he does have a prosthetic leg."

Sage stared at Gavin, speechless. Then at Ethan. She recalled him mounting his horse from the right side and rubbing his knee after they'd dismounted.

"I'm…sorry." She wished she weren't holding the rock so she could bury her face in her hands. "That was insensitive of me."

"Relax. You didn't know."

Ethan had finally stood and was retrieving the rubber mallet he'd dropped. He went on hammering the next fence post as if nothing out of the ordinary had happened.

"I can't believe he still rides," Sage said. "And shoes horses."

"Why not?"

"Because, it…must be hard."

"It is."

"Then why—?"

"This is what we do, Sage. We're cowboys. Always have been and always will be. Losing our ranch, our cattle, our valley to a residential community isn't going to stop us."

He walked away then.

"Gavin, wait!"

He paused. Turned. Only his eyes weren't on her. They narrowed, then widened. "Ethan," he said. "Conner."

His brother and friend looked up from their work. Sage looked, too, and saw what they did.

The mustang. Not a hundred yards from them.

Sage's heart stilled. Before it could start beating again, the jet-black horse tossed his head, whinnied and galloped away, his hooves clattering on the rocks.

So much for her theory that he'd left the area to find a new territory.

"SAGE. HOLD ON A MINUTE." Gavin hurried to catch up with her.

She made it hard for him by not slowing down.

They'd returned to the ranch thirty minutes ago after a long ride back. In that time, they'd unsaddled the horses and put them up, then assembled the equipment for tomorrow. Sage had kept to herself for the most part, both on the ride back to the ranch and afterward.

Gavin let her stew in silence. He had no problem with their differences of opinions, on wild horses, on how to raise their kids and whether or not Ethan should be allowed to live his life in the manner he chose. People didn't always agree.

But when it came to the mustang, he and Sage needed to reach a compromise if they were both going to achieve their goals.

"Okay, I get it. You're mad."

"I'm not mad." She slowed her steps. "It's just that..." They neared the parking area where she'd left her truck that morning. Stopping, she fished her keys from her pocket and depressed the remote door lock. "This whole day has been a disaster."

"Disaster?" He gave her a crooked smile. "Trying, maybe."

She glared at him. "The ride was pure torture."

"I warned you."

"Yes, you did." Her posture sagged. "And then there was Ethan. I totally botched that."

"Come on." He reached for her hand.

"I want to go home." She remained rooted in place, though she didn't withdraw her hand.

He took that as a good sign. "I won't keep you long. I promise."

As they walked, he tried not to dwell on how soft her skin felt or how perfectly her fingers fit inside his. He also ignored the stares from Ethan and Conner and the regular customers milling around the open area. Let them reach their own conclusions. He was too busy enjoying Sage's touch, the first intimate female contact he'd had in over two years.

"Are we going to the house?" she asked.

"The front courtyard. We can talk privately there."

"It's beautiful," she said when they entered the courtyard through a squeaky wrought iron gate.

"My grandfather built it for my grandmother not long after they were married."

A series of three circular steps extended from a large oak door to the spacious courtyard floor. In the center sat an elaborate fountain, though water hadn't run in it for several years. Paloverde and desert willow trees grew side by side outside the low stucco wall, like soldiers standing guard. In the distance, clearly visible between the trees, was Mustang Village.

"It needs some work, I'm afraid." Gavin automatically glanced around.

Many of the red clay tiles were cracked from age, and the trees were in dire need of trimming. The stucco wall hadn't seen a replastering or fresh coat of paint in two decades.

"What's a little disrepair when you have something this charming?"

Sage was being kind. It made him like her all the more. Made him dislike having to let go of her hand.

He escorted her to a pair of chairs tucked in the corner of the courtyard and facing a chipped and weathered Mexican chimenea.

"When my grandparents got older and slowed down," Gavin explained, "my father built these chairs for them. He used leftover boards from the original house my great-grandfather built."

Sage ran her fingertips along an armrest.

Gavin wondered what it might feel like to have those same fingertips caressing him with such delicateness.

He cleared his throat. "It was really more of a shed than a house. There are photographs of it hanging in the hall. My great-grandfather died before the house was finished. Took my granddad five years to complete it."

"That's a great story."

"My father spends a lot of time out here when the weather's nice. And Cassie when she's in a mood." He gestured to the chairs, and Sage sat down.

"When did your family come to the valley?"

"1910." He dropped down beside her. "Ethan, Sierra and I are the fourth generation of Powells to run the ranch."

"Sierra? You have a sister?" Sage looked at him, her brown eyes large and inquisitive.

Gavin was captivated. "Uh...yeah." Sierra. They were talking about Sierra. He had to remember. "She lives in San Francisco."

"How'd she wind up there?"

"That's where the company she works for is based. She visits every chance she gets." He was exaggerating. During the past two years, Sierra had gone to great lengths to put as much physical and emotional distance between her and the rest of them. No one understood why.

"What is it you want to talk about, Gavin?" Sage asked. "I'm guessing it's not your family."

"Actually, it is." He adjusted his hat, buying himself another few seconds. Discussing the past wasn't easy for him. "Twelve years ago, my mother was diagnosed with heart disease. Within months, her health deteriorated. The doctors considered her a good candidate for a transplant. There was only one snag. My parents didn't have adequate health insurance to cover the costs."

He loosened his fingers, which had curled into fists, and continued.

"Dad tried borrowing the money. All the banks turned him down. Ethan and I were too young to be of any financial help. Our neighbor, Bud Duvall, offered to bail us out. At the time, my parents considered him a godsend. He bought all of our land, except for the house, barn, bunkhouse, stables and thirty acres of pasture. He agreed to let us use the land rent free for our cattle operation and then sell it back to us once my mother's heath improved. Interest free."

"Except that didn't happen," Sage guessed.

Gavin swallowed. Even after all these years, Duvall's betrayal still left a bitter taste in his mouth.

"The transplant was successful. But after a few months, my mother's body began rejecting the donor heart. Eventually, an infection developed. She lacked the strength to fight it off. Even if we'd had the money for a second transplant surgery, which we didn't, the transplant board considered her too high a risk. A few weeks later, she died."

"Oh, Gavin." Sage pressed a hand to her lips.

"Cassie was born during the last week of my mother's life. I had no idea that Sandra was even pregnant. We'd only dated a couple months before she broke up with me and didn't see each other after that. I found out about Cassie when she was six weeks old. Sandra's parents hired an attorney, and he showed up at the ranch one day. They wanted to make a deal. I'd give up all custody of Cassie so that Sandra could move with her to Connecticut and live with her parents. In exchange, I wouldn't have to pay any child support."

"And you agreed?"

"Hell, no. But I was young. Twenty-one. My mother had just died. Our cattle business was on the brink of bankruptcy. I wasn't in any position to be a father. As much as I hated to admit it, Sandra's parents were capable of giving Cassie more than I ever could."

"You're her *father*."

"Which is the reason I didn't give up my rights. I paid child support and insisted on visitation."

"Good for you."

"Except I seldom visited. Every three years was all I could afford."

"At least you saw her."

He guessed from her tone she was thinking of Dan.

"I was still a stranger to her."

"Not anymore."

That was debatable. There were times when he and Cassie argued, she looked at him as if she didn't know him from the man behind the deli counter at the local market.

"Mom's death was just the beginning," he continued. "Ethan joined the Marines, his way of coping with the grief. My dad sunk into a deep depression, one he's never come out of. And Sierra, hell, she was just sixteen. Still in high school."

"Which left you to step up and take charge of the family."

"It was my idea to turn the ranch into a public riding stable. We had to do something after Duvall sold our land to an investor."

"I thought you said you had an agreement with him."

"He didn't honor it."

"What about an attorney? Couldn't you have fought the sale?"

"We hired one. Turns out there were a lot of loopholes in the contract. All of them favoring Duvall. My dad had been so anxious to get the money for Mom's transplant surgery, he didn't read the fine print."

Sage reached over and touched Gavin's arm. After a moment, he covered her hand with his.

They sat in silence for several moments before she spoke again.

"You should be commended, Gavin. You've done a great job providing for your family."

"Not that great. We barely get by." His gaze traveled the courtyard, taking in the numerous repairs that needed doing. "I might have been satisfied with that indefinitely. Except something changed this past summer. Something that's made me determined to not only keep the ranch but fix it up into something I'd be proud to pass down to the next generation of Powells."

"Cassie came to live with you."

"Sandra remarried two years ago. They had a baby girl in March. By July, Cassie was here."

"She doesn't like her new sister?"

"Are you serious? You saw her with Isa. She loves kids and, from what Sandra says, doted on the baby. Next to riding horses, the thing she seems to like best is babysitting. She's got quite a nice side business going with some of our customers' children."

"What's wrong then?"

"It's her stepdad. They don't get along. At all. I understand he's strict. Sandra and her parents have always spoiled Cassie. And she's twelve. The school principal is continually reminding me that preadolescence is a challenging age."

"If she is spoiled it doesn't show. She seems like a great kid to me."

"She is a great kid. A little willful at times."

Sage smiled softly. "Like father, like daughter."

There it was again. That radiance warming his insides.

He resisted. Sage wasn't the wisest choice for a romantic relationship even if he was in the market for one.

"Believe it or not, Cassie's the one who asked to come out here. I wish I could say she wanted to see me as much as I did her. The real reason was Sandra and her husband had decided to send Cassie to a boarding school in Massachusetts. She was already attending private school, thanks to her grandparents. I guess they figured boarding school wouldn't be much different."

"Excuse me for being rude, but that sounds, well, insensitive."

"It was. Cassie felt like Sandra chose her husband and new child over her."

"What kid wouldn't feel that way?"

"Rough as it's been on her, I'm grateful. It gave me the chance to be a real dad to her. If she adjusts well and chooses to stay permanently, Sandra's told me she won't object. Of course, she could go back on her word." Gavin had only to remember how low she and her parents had stooped in the past. "But I'm not going to let myself worry about that till it happens."

"I hope it doesn't," Sage said.

Gavin echoed her sentiment. "I know I have a lot to learn about parenting. I say the wrong things, lecture when I should be listening. But I love her and have sworn to do right by her. Give her everything a kid her age needs."

"I still don't see how any of this—"

"With the mustang, I'll be able to bring in more revenue.

For Cassie. And to make this place into something other than a ramshackle old house and a falling down barn."

"I do understand how important it is for a parent to provide for their child."

"It's more than that. Powell Ranch isn't just a home. It's our legacy."

"Like being cowboys and keeping the tradition alive," Sage said thoughtfully.

"Exactly."

"You're counting an awful lot on that mustang."

"I'm also counting on your help capturing him."

Her expression hardened. "And Dan for his financial backing."

So much for winning her over. "I know what I'm asking of you isn't easy. To work with your ex-husband—"

"We were never married." Dark emotion flashed in her eyes.

"Sorry." He shouldn't have assumed, especially given his own circumstances. "Dan's loss."

She regarded him for several seconds, th the valley below. "It is really pretty here. Even with all ne houses and buildings. I can see why you'd fight to keep it."

He read between the lines. "You can't put your differences with Dan aside."

"Actually, I think I could. Him, on the other hand…" She shrugged. "Doubtful."

"He was agreeable when I talked to him yesterday."

"He won't be much longer. And I'm not sure you will, either."

"What's going on, Sage?"

"I didn't come to Mustang Valley solely for the horse. Or to arrange for Isa to meet her father." She smoothed her ponytail, the gesture a nervous one. "Dan owes me, owes Isa, a considerable amount of back child support."

He waited for her to finish, his stomach tightening with each second.

"I'm going to collect it. Do whatever's necessary. Like you are for Cassie. Things might get awkward and unpleasant."

Gavin could see where they would.

"It's possible…" She rose. "No, I'll be honest with you. It's very likely you'll be involved."

"How?" He also rose.

"I wish there was another way. You have no idea how much. But I have to think of Isa. She has a right to the money Dan owes her."

"Tell me."

"You'll be receiving garnishment papers from the state soon."

Gavin sank back into his chair. "How soon?"

"I'm guessing by the end of the week."

He could easily imagine Dan's reaction.

Sage placed a hand on Gavin's shoulder. "I hope your agreement with Dan is in writing and ironclad."

It wasn't, but he didn't tell her that and barely noticed when she walked away.

Chapter Seven

The ride to the canyon on Sunday was every bit as demanding for Sage as the previous day. Not so for the men. Ethan and Conner, leastwise. Their spirits soared as the four of them navigated the same steep trails and jagged terrain. When conversation was possible, they talked about what techniques they'd employ to capture the mustang, confident of returning to the ranch in a few hours with their prize in tow.

Sage said little. Neither did Gavin. Not to her, anyway.

Okay, she deserved the silent treatment after the bombshell she'd dropped on him yesterday. If he'd just talk to her, she'd apologize. Tell him how she hated putting him and his family in a bad position. They were innocent bystanders. Like her and Isa. Victims of Dan's selfishness. She had no choice except to report any possible payees to the Child Support Enforcement Agency.

A turn on the trail tickled her memory. Up ahead, she recognized the entrance to the box canyon and silently rejoiced. Ahead of her, the three men simultaneously craned their necks to see into the canyon. Sage did, too.

"You spot him?" Gavin asked Ethan. He was leading the gelding, the lone packhorse they'd brought along.

"Not yet."

The horses increased their pace, no doubt picking up on their riders' eager anticipation to reach their destination. Sage patted Avaro's neck. The mare had once more started out the morning acting up, then quickly calmed, for which Sage and her sore muscles were grateful.

Five minutes later, they finally had a clear, if distant, view of the mares in their makeshift pen.

From what Sage could tell, there was no sign of the mustang. She tried to stave off disappointment. He could be hiding beneath the rock ledge or behind a rise.

Gavin reined in his horse, causing Sage to stop, as well. He reached behind him, removed a pair of binoculars from his saddlebags and lifted them to his eyes. After several moments of scanning the canyon in every direction, he lowered the binoculars.

No one asked what he'd seen. The answer was clearly written on his face.

The mustang wasn't in the canyon.

Sage rolled her sore shoulders and sighed. All this work for nothing. She should have insisted on contacting the city about using the ATVs. Now, they had no choice.

"How are the mares?" Ethan asked.

"They look okay from here."

As the group started out again, the mares spotted them and began whinnying, their high-pitched calls echoing through the canyon. Avaro and the gelding both answered back.

Near the pen, they dismounted and tethered their horses.

Conner was the first to reach the mares, who pressed eagerly against the sagging lines. "Come here!" Motioning everyone over, he pointed at the ground.

There was no need to clarify. Sage could see what had raised his interest. Hoofprints. Lots of them. Outside the pen and all around.

The mustang might not be here now, but he'd returned at some point during the night.

Gavin pulled on one of the pen's lines, which hung loosely in his hand. "He tried to get to the mares."

"Or they tried to get out," Ethan said.

"Probably both," Conner added.

Gavin raised his gaze to the canyon walls. "You can bet he's not far."

"And that he'll be back."

"I'm counting on it."

Conner meandered over to where the bottom line was anchored to the thick root of a shrub growing between two boulders and began untying it.

Sage assumed to disassemble the pen.

Shouldn't someone locate the halters first so the mares wouldn't get loose?

Gavin checked the level of water they'd left for the mares, absently stroking the head of the nearest one.

Sage waited for him to dump the remaining water so they could load the tub and take it home with everything else.

Ethan returned to the packhorse, his limp every bit as pronounced as before, and started unfastening the ropes securing the pack saddles. "Sage, how about a hand with this?"

She hurried to help him, mentally calculating how long it would take them to pack up and get back on the trail. How long until she could soak away her aches and pains in another hot bath.

Together, she and Ethan lifted the heavy plastic tarp. Beneath it, in the panniers, was a five-gallon jug of water, a large sack of pellets, additional line and some of the same equipment they'd brought yesterday.

Sage stared at the items in disbelief.

"I thought…" Words failed her.

"What?" Ethan looked at her over the horse's back, his expression innocent.

Irritation flared. Were he and his brother taking her for

a fool? Then it struck her. "You're leaving the mares here another night."

Gavin came up beside her.

She faced him, accusation in her voice. "You planned this all along."

"We considered the possibility it might take more than one night to lure the mustang into the canyon and came prepared."

"That's not what you told me."

He reached past her and dug into the pannier, removing the sack of pellets. Hefting it into his arms, he carried it to the makeshift pen.

"I can't come back tomorrow." Sage chased after him.

He set the sack on the ground and straightened. "Why not? You said you had a whole week. It's only been four days."

Sage swallowed. She wasn't going to tell him about the paternity test and the appointment she'd made for her and Isa. "I have a previous commitment."

"All day?"

"In the morning."

"Fine. We'll ride out after lunch. Ethan, can you get someone to cover your classes?"

"I'll ask Rebecca."

Gavin returned his attention to Sage. "Will that give you enough time for your commitment?"

His matter-of-fact attitude irked her. They were supposed to have the mustang by now.

She should have known it wouldn't be that easy.

"You can bring Isa with you to the ranch." He bent down and stepped between the lines, entering the pen. The mares immediately crowded around him, sensing that food was coming. "My dad will keep an eye on her. Cassie can take her riding again on Chico."

"No." Sage quashed the panic bubbling in her and hissed, "What if Dan's there?"

"He won't be."

"And you know this for sure?"

Thankfully, Gavin lowered his voice. "I talked to him last night. He's going to Casa Grande for the day to meet with a potential client."

Well, that much was a relief at least.

Gavin poured the pellets into the trough. The mares, unable to wait, reached in for bites.

Sage reconsidered as she watched. The paternity test might be stressful for Isa. If so, an afternoon at the ranch would do her good.

"What if the mustang isn't here again tomorrow?" she asked.

Gavin climbed out of the pen and straightened to his full height. Sage had to tip her head back to look him in the eyes. Those killer blue eyes. She wasn't sure what disconcerted her the most, his height, his proximity or the way in which he studied her.

"Then we'll come back Tuesday."

"On ATV's."

His brows drew together. "We've had this discussion already."

"I think we should reopen it."

To her annoyance, he walked away from her, *again,* and back toward the packhorse.

Ethan and Conner, busy repairing the makeshift pen, stopped to stare openly at Gavin and Sage.

Rather than go after him, *again,* she, called out, "Like you said, I only have a few days left. We need to make the most of them."

"Forget it. The city won't move fast enough. Too much red tape."

"I'll see if my supervisor can expedite the request."

"No."

She did go after him then. "Gavin, this isn't a one-man operation. You don't get to make all the decisions."

He stopped unloading the equipment and glowered at her. Glowered! "I know these mountains. Every inch. And I know this horse. I've spent four months tracking his every move. You couldn't capture him with ATVs if you had a whole fleet of them. Do you have any idea how big this mountain range is?"

"No, but—"

"Over ninety-thousand acres. That's a lot of ground to cover. And I guarantee that horse can go places you can't begin to on an ATV."

Despite his annoying tone, what he said made sense. If only he weren't so stubborn.

"Fine. One more day. But if that mustang isn't here tomorrow afternoon, I'm calling my supervisor." She had no intention of spending her entire vacation in Mustang Valley chasing a horse that obviously didn't want to be chased.

Gavin smiled. The same devastatingly handsome smile he'd given her when they first met. To her embarrassment, a fluttery sensation in her middle left her mildly weak-kneed.

This was bad indeed.

She thought she heard one of the other men chuckle. When she looked over, Ethan was coughing into his hand. Ignoring him *and* Gavin, she threw herself into helping unpack.

Soon, they were done. The mares, tended and secure in their repaired pen, weren't happy to be left behind and whinnied their protests. Sage searched the canyon as they rode out, hoping for a repeat appearance of the mustang. She wasn't alone.

Unfortunately, wherever he was, nearby or not, he remained well hidden.

Sundays were evidently a slow day for the ranch. A few people were grooming or walking out their horses, and a pair of teenagers rode in the arena.

Gavin joined Sage just as she was putting Avaro up in her stall. Though he appeared friendly enough, she doubted their truce would last.

"I'm not trying to make your job harder," he said when she'd shut the stall door.

"If that's an apology, it needs a little work."

"It's not."

Was this irritating man really the same one who'd left her weak-kneed earlier? "What do you want, Gavin?"

"To make a deal with you. If the mustang isn't in the canyon tomorrow, I won't object to you calling your supervisor."

"Then you agree we can use ATVs."

"No. Only that the BLM can contact the city."

Realization dawned. "You think they'll refuse our request."

"There's a good chance of it. The city isn't known for bending the rules."

"I guess we'll see." Sage spun on her heels. She didn't get far.

Gavin quickly fell into step beside her. "Okay, I'm a jerk. I admit it. But you're being selfish."

That brought her to a halt. "Selfish?"

"You want to avoid Dan, and you have every good reason. But that's no excuse to force a method of capturing the mustang on me that not only has an ice cube's chance in hell of working, it's damaging to the environment and dangerous to the wildlife."

"This is getting us nowhere." She refused to acknowledge the grain of truth in what he said.

"There's a trail ride and picnic this afternoon. We have it every third Sunday of the month for our customers and their guests. Everyone brings their own food and drinks. We head out about four, ride for an hour, stop, eat and then come back, usually by seven or seven-thirty."

"That's nice, but what does it have to do with the mustang?"

"Yesterday you mentioned the view of the city at night. This would be your chance to see it."

She blinked in astonishment. "Are you inviting me?"

"And Isa."

"Why?" she blustered.

"Because I thought maybe if we...socialized some, it might improve our working relationship."

She almost laughed. "You're joking."

He shook his head. "Not at all."

"Let me think about it."

"Take your time."

He left her then, and she watched him stride leisurely out of the stables, the impressive width of his broad shoulders filling the jacket he wore. She'd watched those shoulders for two days now on the trail.

It wasn't a hardship, then or now.

Was she crazy to even consider going on the trail ride? Her weary body screamed yes.

Except Isa would love it. Have the time of her life. Sage had yet to tell her about the paternity test tomorrow, waiting for the perfect opportunity. Of course, she was procrastinating.

She could do it this afternoon, on the way back to the ranch. If she used the right words, downplayed the test, played up the trail ride, Isa might respond better. Be less scared.

And maybe "socializing" with Gavin *would* improve their relationship.

She hurried out of the stables. When she found him and

accepted his invitation, her repeat reaction to his sexy, satisfied grin had her reconsidering her motives and cursing her vulnerability.

SAGE STILL HADN'T TOLD Isa about the paternity test, and they would be at Powell Ranch in less than twenty minutes. She started to speak, only to have her courage desert her. How did one explain to a six-year-old that her father insisted on proof she was his biological daughter?

One didn't, obviously, and neither would Sage. She'd give some other reason for the test. A simplified version of the truth Isa would understand.

As her daughter prattled on about Chico and seeing Cassie, another mile came and went. Sage stared at the road, at the passing landscape, half listening.

A memory from two years ago suddenly sprang into sharp focus. Isa had fallen from the swing set at preschool and broken her arm. The bones hadn't healed correctly and after ten days, the orthopedic surgeon recommended rebreaking the arm.

It would hurt. A lot. Isa would cry. But it had to be done or she would be left with limited range of motion in that arm. Preparing Isa for the procedure had been one of the worst times in Sage's life. But then, thirty minutes later, it was over. Isa, sucking on a lollipop, sported a pink fiberglass cast of which she was quite proud. A week later, she'd forgotten all about the pain.

Maybe it would be the same with the paternity test.

Sage turned off Pima Road and headed east on Dynamite. Less than fifteen minutes until they reached the ranch.

"*Mija*, Mama has to talk to you about something important."

Isa stopped her animated chatter. The stuffed cat, named Purr-o, came to rest in her lap. "What?"

"We, you and I, have an appointment tomorrow morning."

"Where?"

"At a testing facility." *Smile,* she told herself, *and relax.*

"We have to take a test?"

"Yes."

"Like a spelling test?"

"More like a medical test."

"I'm going to the doctor?" Fear widened Isa's eyes.

"No, not a doctor. I swear." Sage reached over and stroked Isa's hair. "And the test won't hurt at all. Someone called a technician will just take a small sample from both of us."

"What kind of sample?"

She went on to explain the procedure in terms Isa could comprehend. "It'll only take a few minutes, and I'll be right with you the whole time."

Isa hugged Purr-o to her chest. "Do I have to?"

Here was the question Sage had dreaded the most.

"You remember Mama telling you about the money Papa pays for you?" She'd briefly mentioned the child support to Isa, omitting the part about Dan not paying for four years. "We need to have the test done in order to get the payments."

Isa's small brow knitted in confusion.

"You see, the test results will go to…" Sage paused, worried she might be overexplaining. "Will go to Papa."

"Why?"

"He asked, and I said yes."

Isa scowled and stuck out her bottom lip.

"Really, sweetie pie, the test won't hurt a bit. Afterward, when your papa pays the money, I'll buy you a pony."

Bribing her child. Could she be a worse parent?

"Will I get to meet Papa?"

Another question Sage had dreaded and one she was even less ready to answer.

"Soon. Maybe while we're here visiting Tia Anna and Tio Roberto."

First bribing and then lying to Isa. Sage truly was a terrible parent.

"Can you call him?" Isa asked out of the blue.

"What?"

"Papa. Can you call him and tell him I want to see him?"

Sage took her eyes off the road to study Isa. "Are you sure?"

Isa nodded vigorously.

"O…kay."

"When?"

"Well, I—"

"Now?"

What would she say to Dan? What would she say to Isa when Dan refused?

"Please, Mama."

With shaking fingers, Sage picked up her phone and dialed Dan's number. Relief flooded her when the call went straight to voice mail. Then shame at her relief.

"Dan," she said after the beep, "this is Sage. Call me as soon as you get this message. It's about Isa. Sorry, *mija,*" she said, gratefully disconnecting.

The delay was temporary, she reminded herself. Soon enough, she'd have to deal with Dan. If only to keep her promise to Isa.

"Are you excited about the trail ride?"

"Yeah, I guess."

Isa's response couldn't be more glum. The poor kid was having way more thrown at her than she deserved.

Sage pressed a hand to her chest and the knot of misery

lodged there. She didn't cry a lot. Being a single mother, the sole support of her child, financially and emotionally, had toughened her up. But the past few days had severely weakened her defenses.

"What kind of pony will I get?" Isa asked, her tone marginally brighter. "Will it be a mustang?"

"Probably not." Sage fought the tears pricking her eyes. "Mustangs are big. And too wild for a little girl."

"Chico's big."

"But he's old. And very tame."

"Like Black Beauty." The movie was one of Isa's favorites.

"A little."

She concentrated on the end of the month, when she and Isa would head home in Show Low, with the first of the delinquent child support payments in the mail. She didn't consider Dan and his unlikely visit with Isa, having heard his fabricated excuses once too often.

By the time they reached the entrance to Powell Ranch, Sage was dry-eyed.

"There's Cassie and Blue." Isa bounced excitedly in her seat, her former happy self once more.

Thank goodness.

Cassie waved them over. Sage pulled to a stop and pushed the button to lower Isa's window. "Can Isa go with you while I park?"

"Sure. Come on, pip-squeak."

Isa bailed out of the truck, charging Cassie and throwing her arms around the older girl. Blue, connected to Cassie by a leash, jumped up on Isa's legs and begged for attention. Isa bent and scooped him up in her arms.

Her delighted laughter floated through the open window, acting like a balm on Sage's bruised emotions.

She drove slowly to the parking area behind the barn,

carefully avoiding all the people and horses. The trail ride and picnic was obviously very popular with the ranch clientele. She spotted Ethan and Conner. Gavin, however, was nowhere in sight.

Just as well. Sage didn't want another confrontation with him.

Slipping the truck into an empty space, she shut off the engine and opened the door. Rather than get immediately out, she waited, needing one last minute to compose herself before facing people.

Flipping down the sun visor, she checked her reflection in the small mirror.

Wonderful. Her mascara had run and left black smudges beneath her eyes. She searched among the pile of toys and folders and CD cases for a tissue. There was none. Using the cuff of her shirtsleeve, she dabbed at her ruined makeup.

Later, she would find humor in the situation. At least no one was nearby to see her.

"You okay?"

She started at the sound of Gavin's voice. Where had he come from?

"Great," she mumbled, issuing what she hoped was another forgivable lie.

"You don't look great." He stepped closer, in between her and the open truck door.

"Allergies. Something must be in bloom."

"Here." He removed a red kerchief from his back pocket. It was clean and folded in a tidy square.

She turned it over in her hand, hating the idea of messing it and impressed by his sensitivity. "Thank you, but—"

"Go on," he urged. Kindly. Sweetly.

It was a little more than Sage could handle. Even as she wiped at her eyes, fresh tears spilled. Then a sob escaped, which she quickly swallowed. She could not, *would* not, break down. Not in front of Gavin.

Before she quite knew what was happening, she was being lifted from the truck and onto the ground...then into Gavin's arms.

Every shred of common sense she possessed urged her to step away. She hardly knew him. Not really. One personal conversation didn't make them intimate friends.

Except his arms had settled comfortably around her and held her close with just the right amount of tenderness.

"Everything's going to be all right," he murmured in her ear.

"You don't know," she protested, a catch in her voice.

"I don't have to know. You're a strong woman. You'll get through it, whatever it is."

How long since a man, since anyone, had held her and offered her comfort? Been a shelter during a storm?

Maybe Dan, in the early days of their relationship. She honestly couldn't remember. Gavin, with his broad chest providing a very nice, very welcoming place for her to lay her head, was wiping away every memory of every man that came before him.

His hand drifted to the middle of her back and pressed lightly. Sage's own hands rested awkwardly at the sides of his denim jacket. For one brief second, she allowed herself to imagine what it would be like to circle his middle with her arms and nestle fully against him.

Crazy. And highly inappropriate. Certainly not the kind of thoughts a crying woman had about a man.

Except she wasn't crying anymore.

"Sorry about that," she murmured, and slowly began to disengage herself.

"Don't be." He halted her by tucking a finger beneath

her chin, tilting her head up and bringing his mouth down on hers.

Her arms, no longer awkward and indecisive, clung to him as she gave herself over to what quickly became the most incredible kiss of her life.

her gaze slid to her lips and then . . . dragging his mouth close to hers . . . nothing, no sound, save for and . . . Gavin wasn't . . . he gave because he thought so or . . . because the most breathtaking kiss of his life.

Chapter Eight

Kissing Sage hadn't been Gavin's intention when he first spotted her sitting in her truck, struggling not to cry. He was only going to ask if he could help.

But then he caught sight of her face and her lost expression, completely unlike the capable and fearless woman he'd come to know. Taking her into his arms, on the other hand, had been a conscious act. If there was ever someone who'd needed holding, it was Sage in that moment.

Now, leaning in, drawing her close...that was something he couldn't explain and didn't want to.

Not while they were fused together, hungry for each other.

Her lips, soft and pliant and incredibly delicious, molded perfectly to his. Then, they parted. That was all it took for Gavin's thinly held control to snap.

Wrapping his arms more tightly around her, he angled his head and tasted her fully. She responded by pressing herself flush against him, her fingers curling into the hair at the base of his neck. He seared the feel and taste of her into his memory because he would not soon forget this day.

Or her.

Stopping occurred to him. After all, there were people—lots of them—within a few dozen yards of her truck. But the next second she rose up on her tiptoes and traced the outline of his jaw with her fingertips. Gavin quit trying to be responsible for his actions and worrying about proprieties. Instead, he let his instincts take over. They served him well.

When he thought he couldn't possibly get more lost in the moment, want a woman more than he did her, the inevitable occurred.

They were interrupted.

"Mama, Mama!"

Gavin reluctantly released Sage just as Isa came racing across the parking area, Cassie and Blue not far behind.

"Over here, *mija*."

"What are you doing?" Isa's large brown eyes traveled from her mother to Gavin.

"Getting our food." Sage reached into the truck's cab and removed a small soft-sided cooler and two plastic bottles of vitamin water.

"Can I carry it?"

"Sure."

Isa took the cooler and bottles. She didn't appear to notice the vivid flush staining her mother's cheek or the unsteadiness in her voice.

Gavin did and grinned. He couldn't help it. He rather enjoyed knowing he was the cause of her discomfort.

Sage scowled at him.

He didn't let it faze him. She'd participated in their kiss every bit as much as he had. And enjoyed it every bit as much, too.

His grin died when he caught Cassie staring at them with a much-too-knowing look on her face.

Shoot. He might have some explaining to do later. For now, he chose to pretend nothing was out of the ordinary. Not easy to do when the past five minutes had been extraordinary.

"What did you bring to eat?" he asked Isa.

"Leftover chicken, fruit salad, tortillas and chocolate cookies," she answered proudly.

"Enough for me, too?"

The little girl looked dismayed. "I don't know."

"Don't worry." He tugged on her earlobe. "I was joking with you."

"You can have one of my cookies."

"Now, that's an offer I won't refuse."

Sage slammed the truck door shut and pocketed her keys. "We should probably get going."

Isa trudged out ahead of them, the cooler slung over one shoulder and the water bottles clutched to her chest. Cassie walked along beside her, Blue obediently trotting at her heels.

Gavin tried not to read too much into Cassie's silence. It hadn't occurred to him to speculate how his daughter might react to a new woman in his life since the prospect had been nonexistent until now.

Considering that Sage was leaving soon *and* was his business partner's ex, those chances were still pretty nonexistent.

Two more last-minute arrivals pulled into the parking area. The occupants of the vehicles waved as they hurried into the stables to saddle their horses. Already riders were assembled in the open area in front of the arena, some mounted, some gathered in small groups. All of them excited.

Gavin liked the monthly trail rides and picnics, and not just because they were his brainchild. Something about them reminded him a little of when he was young, back before his mother got sick and Mustang Village was built. Families from various ranches in the area would gather together a few times a year for similar trail rides and picnics.

Gavin spotted his brother helping one of their regular students, and his thoughts turned contemplative.

Also in those long-ago days, Ethan had both legs and his

best friend was Clay Duvall. Gavin remembered the two boys, no more than eight or nine, fishing in the river while everyone else ate and relaxed under the shade of nearby trees.

Now Ethan wore a prosthetic leg, their mother was gone and neither of them had spoken to Duvall since his father sold the Powells' land to the investor.

Times change, and all the wishing in the world couldn't restore what had been taken from them. The best Gavin could do, for himself and his family, was take whatever life dealt them and adapt.

Until he was on solid financial ground, until his and his family's future more secure, until he knew if Cassie was living with him permanently or returning to Connecticut, he had no right getting involved with *any* woman, much less Sage.

But then, there was the kiss.

"We should talk about what happened back there," she said.

"Why spoil it with talk?"

"It was a mistake."

"There you go."

"Gavin."

He chuckled at her exasperated tone, which earned him another scowl.

"I don't want you to get the wrong idea."

He had a lot of ideas at the moment, none of which felt wrong despite his earlier attempt to convince himself otherwise.

"Kissing men I barely know isn't something I do."

"So, I'm special?"

She groaned.

"Relax, Sage, it was no big deal."

"It wasn't?"

Her dismay made him grin.

"Are you kidding?" He came to a halt. When she did, too,

and he had her full attention, he said in a sober voice, "I can't remember when anything was a bigger deal."

For a moment, her eyes softened, and he saw what could be between them if things were different. But then she closed her eyes and drew in a breath. When she next looked at him, the resolve was back—as was an emotional shield he didn't have to see to know was there.

GAVIN AND SAGE FOUND the girls in the stables.

"Hey, Dad!" Cassie had already saddled old Chico and Barbie Doll, her favorite horse, well before Isa arrived so they'd be ready to go. "Can Isa and I ride around while you get ready?"

"It's up to her mom."

"Sure." Sage lifted Isa onto Chico. "Don't go far."

Cassie tucked Blue into the front of her jacket, adjusted the zipper over his head, then mounted. No sooner was she seated than the puppy's head popped out.

"You be careful you don't drop him," Gavin warned.

Cassie tried to push Blue back inside her jacket. He resisted. What would she do when he got bigger?

Gavin refused to think about Cassie returning to her mother's after the holidays and not seeing Blue grow up.

"Maybe Isa and I can go with you tomorrow to capture the wild mustang."

"You have school."

"Uh-uh. Fall break."

Oh, yeah.

He was inclined to let Cassie come along. His grandfather and father had taken him on rides in the mountains when he was much younger than twelve. Isa, he was less sure about.

"Can we, Mama?" she asked.

"I'm afraid not, sweetie pie."

"Please," she begged.

"No. You're too young."

Gavin recognized the tone. It was the same one his mother had used on him when further arguing was useless.

He hesitated telling Cassie she could come along if Isa couldn't.

Fortunately, Cassie spoke up.

"It's okay, Isa," she said good-naturedly. "You can stay with me. We'll go riding. And afterward, you can help me clean stalls."

Isa was appeased, judging by her happy smile.

Sage wasn't. "Okay. But not without adult supervision."

"My dad will watch them," he offered.

"Grandpa?" Cassie's mouth fell open.

"I'll ask him." It wasn't easy getting his father out of the house, but he had a soft spot for Cassie who, Gavin suspected, reminded him of Sierra.

"Fifteen minutes!" Ethan hollered from where he stood at the entrance to the stable. "Fifteen minutes!"

"We'd better hurry and saddle up."

They joined the group just in the nick of time. Gavin hoped Ethan remembered to bring their picnic dinner. If not, Isa's cookie might be all he got to eat until they returned.

Duty dictated he check on all the riders, not just Sage, and there were quite a few of them. Thirty-four, he determined after a quick head count. This was their largest monthly ride yet.

For the first time since he and his family had decided to turn what was left of their ranch into a riding stables, Gavin dared to believe he might actually carve out a decent life for himself and Cassie.

Once he had ownership of the mustang, that was.

The riders went mostly single file through the gate leading from the back pasture to the trailhead. Ethan rode in front, Conner in the middle and Gavin brought up the rear. Just as he was dismounting to shut the gate after the last rider, he noticed Sage.

Avaro was acting up again. Worse than earlier in the day. Ears pinned back, she bared her teeth at the horse beside her and threatened to kick the one behind her. Sage did a prompt and thorough job of removing Avaro a safe distance away. Holding the mare in position, she waited for Gavin.

"It might be best if I rode with you."

He was happy to oblige.

Spotting a fresh wound on Avaro's neck near her shoulder, he asked, "What happened there?"

"I think she got in a fight with her neighbor in the next stall. One I'm sure she started and that won't be her last." Sage sighed wearily.

Some mares were unbothered when they came into heat. Others, like Avaro, became cranky and aggressive.

"We have a small pen near the pasture. We could put her in there if you want."

Sage considered his suggestion, then shook her head. "She doesn't like to be alone. And she's something of an escape artist. Twice, when I've put her by herself, she's jumped the fence in order to be with other horses."

No small feat considering her compact stature.

"Why don't we put her in with the mares? They're less likely to agitate her than the geldings in the stables."

They'd reached the branch of the trail that would take them into the mountains.

"Do you mind? I don't think she'll bother the mares or foals."

Gavin agreed. Avaro was hardly paying any attention to Shasta.

"If it doesn't work, we can always put her back in a stall."

"Thank you." Sage's expression had gone soft again.

It was fast becoming Gavin's favorite one.

"About…the kiss."

He smiled. "You really are going to talk about it."

"Don't you think we should?"

"Tomorrow. When we return from capturing the mustang."

"Or tonight when we get back from the ride."

She drove a hard bargain.

Gavin was about to tell her as much when his cell phone rang. Reception was iffy out here so he reined Shasta to a stop. Sage also stopped, her glance traveling ahead to the riders stretched out in front of them. Isa and old Chico were plodding along. Cassie rode directly behind them, chatting with another girl. All was well.

Removing his phone from his pocket, he checked the display. All was evidently not well. His glance cut to Sage, then he flipped the phone open.

"Hello, Dan."

She sat straighter in the saddle, her lips compressed to a thin line.

"Is it true?" Dan demanded. "Are Sage and Isa on the trail ride with you?"

"Yes." Gavin didn't tell Dan exactly how close Sage was to him.

Dan swore in Spanish. "I agreed not to go on the roundup when you asked me. Nothing was ever said about them participating in ranch activities."

One of his clients must have mentioned the woman from the BLM. There'd been quite a stir about Sage and the mustang the past few days.

"It's no big deal," Gavin explained patiently. "When we got back from the mountains today, I invited them on the trail ride. Simply being hospitable."

"I don't want that bitch and her kid anywhere near that ranch unless it's to go after the mustang, you hear me?"

There was much in what Dan said that infuriated Gavin, starting with calling Sage a derogatory name and ending with the barely concealed threat.

"We'll talk tomorrow." Unable to continue the conversation, he disconnected and pocketed his phone.

"Like I said—" Sage gathered her reins "—kissing was a mistake." Nudging her mare into a walk, she set out after the others.

It wasn't, Gavin thought, following at a much slower pace.

But his choice of business partners was sure starting to look like one.

GAVIN PERCHED ON A ROCK at the outskirts of the circle, eating the cookie Isa had given him. Everywhere he looked, horses were tethered to bushes and low hanging branches. This spot was one the group often chose for their picnics because of the ample level ground and breathtaking view.

The sun was at that moment slipping behind Pinnacle Peak. From where he sat, the top of the peak glowed a brilliant russet as if a fire burned within its core. Gavin had witnessed this eye-popping spectacle many times, but it never failed to amaze and inspire him.

Ethan limped over and claimed the rock next to Gavin's. The past few days had been hard on him. Fortunately, he was physically fit, thanks to the Marines and years playing sports and rodeoing before that.

Though his brother would be the last to complain, Gavin wasn't fooled. Ethan hurt and should probably see his doctor. Gavin kept his mouth shut, however. Experience had taught him his brother would go when he was damn good and ready.

"What time are we heading out tomorrow?" he asked, passing Gavin a bottled water.

"Between noon and one," he answered. "Sage has some business to take care of in the morning."

Ethan rubbed his knee where the prosthetic leg was attached. "Okay. But we have to get back at a halfway decent hour."

"You have plans?"

"I do."

His brother's mysterious comings and goings were increasing in frequency. "How soon until you're ready to tell me what it is you're up to?"

"Soon."

Gavin respected his brother's privacy, but he was also worried. "Be careful."

"I am." Ethan's gaze darted to Sage, who was chatting with a middle-aged couple. Nearby, Cassie supervised as children took turns playing with Blue. "I take it you and Sage are getting along better."

"What makes you say that?"

"I noticed you earlier at her truck. Looked to me like you were well on the way to resolving your differences."

"How much did you see?"

"Enough."

"She was upset. Dan's been giving her grief."

Ethan took a long swig of his water. "You sure you want to get involved with her? Dan's our financial backing. They may not be together anymore, but that doesn't mean he'll be okay with you dating her."

"We're not going to date."

"Then explain the kiss."

"It was an accident."

"I don't think he'll be any less angry with you just because your mouth *accidentally* collided with hers."

Ethan was right. "Dan called me when we were riding out. He's furious that Sage and Isa came along on the ride."

"What are you going to do?"

"Not let things get out of hand."

"Is that possible?"

"It's what Sage wants."

"I'm not hearing a lot of conviction in your voice."

His brother could always read him better than anyone else.

"Even if we weren't counting on Dan's money, I'd still steer clear of Sage."

"Why?"

"She lives in Show Low for starters," Gavin said quietly. His family, he knew, was frequently the topic of conversation with their customers despite his efforts to keep their private life just that.

"She can move."

"Her job is there."

"She can find a new one. Or transfer."

"I'm not in a position to date."

"Because of Cassie?"

"Partly."

Ethan snorted dismissively. "I'm pretty sure Sage likes kids."

"I have nothing to offer a woman. Financially," he clarified when Ethan started to object.

"How do you know money's important to her?"

"It's important to me." Gavin was a holdover from the dark ages, according to some people, but he'd been raised to believe a man should provide for his wife and children.

"There's another solution," Ethan said contemplatively, "if you really care for her."

Gavin's curiosity got the better of him. "What?"

"Sell the ranch."

He could tell by Ethan's grave expression, this was no joke. "Forget it."

"Before you get bent out of shape, listen to me." Ethan leaned forward, his elbows propped on his thighs, the empty bottle of water dangling between his legs. "Dad has no interest in the ranch anymore. Neither does Sierra. I'm only here because you need help."

Was that true? Gavin had always assumed Ethan's love for their family's home ran as deep as his.

"I don't have the authority to sell the ranch. It's in all of our names." Their father had deeded the remaining property equally to Gavin, Ethan and Sierra a year after their mother had died.

"I'd sign off if you want to sell," Ethan answered. "And I'm pretty sure Sierra would, too."

"No."

"I'm just saying, if you ever wanted to move. Like to Show Low."

"No," Gavin answered more emphatically. He'd buy out his brother and sister before selling the ranch. Maybe that was what they secretly wanted. "Are you tired of working with me?"

Ethan shrugged. "It's not like I'm doing anything else. Or *can* do anything else." He chuckled mirthlessly. "Not much call for one-legged bull riders or police officers." Those were the two professions Ethan had considered before joining the Marines. "It occurred to me, if we sold the ranch, maybe we could all start fresh."

What Gavin heard was "quit fighting a losing battle."

"I don't want to sell the ranch," he said. "Not yet. If the stud and breeding business tanks, then maybe I'll…" The words stuck in his throat. Gnashing his teeth together, he forced them out. "Think about it."

"First things first." Ethan clapped Gavin on the back and rose. "Gotta capture the mustang."

Gavin also rose. Evening was falling fast, and it was well past time to head back. "All the more reason to keep things professional with Sage."

Except it wouldn't be easy. As he walked the picnic area, supervising the cleanup and helping the younger riders onto their horses, he couldn't keep his eyes off her or his mind from reliving their kiss.

Chapter Nine

Ten minutes into the return ride, Avaro started acting up again. After she bit yet another horse, Sage removed them from the line and waited until all the riders had gone ahead. Then, like before, fell into place beside Gavin.

Being with Shasta made little difference. Avaro pranced and fought the bit until sweat broke out on her neck and foam gathered at her mouth.

"I don't understand," Sage complained to Gavin. "She wants to be with the other horses, then kicks and bites them."

"It doesn't help that we have two stallions at the ranch."

"Probably not." Sage tugged on the reins. "I can't wait to get home."

"I'm sorry your trip isn't turning out the way you hoped it would."

"It's not your fault."

"You sure? You've been mad at me more than once."

She hadn't been mad earlier when they were kissing. Maybe at Isa for interrupting them.

"Dan's insisting on a paternity test. He's suddenly decided Isa may not be his."

"Is that what upset you?"

"I told her about the test on the way here."

"That must have been hard."

"It was awful. There's no chance the test won't come back positive. I'm just furious at Dan for putting us through it."

Avaro chose that moment to rear on her hind legs and thrash out with her front ones.

Fortunately, no other riders were nearby, except for Gavin who acted quickly and turned Shasta away.

Sage was mortified. And annoyed. Mostly at herself. She should have known better than to bring Avaro on a ride when the horse was in heat.

"There's another trail going back to the ranch," Gavin suggested when Sage once again had control of the horse— temporarily, she was sure. "We can take it if you want."

"Good idea."

"The trail's a little rough," he warned. "And it'll be dark soon."

"I can handle it."

He nodded. "Wait here for me. I'll tell Ethan."

"Can Cassie watch Isa? I hate to impose—"

"She won't mind." Gavin nudged Shasta into a trot.

"Tell her I'll pay," Sage hollered after him.

Avaro immediately started to prance in place and whinny. At one point, Sage noticed something moving from the corner of her eye. She scanned the eastern rise. A dark shape moved along the rocky ledge. In the next instant, Avaro distracted Sage by tugging hard on the reins. When Sage next looked at the rise, whatever was there, if there'd been anything at all, was gone.

Shadows, she told herself. The last smoky rays of daylight dancing across the mountains.

Gavin returned, and Avaro promptly quieted.

Soon, they came upon a narrow trail Sage hadn't noticed before. It was, as Gavin had informed her, steep and rough.

At the bottom, the ground gave way, probably washed out from a recent flash flood. Gavin's mare cleared the ditch effortlessly, landing solidly on the other side. He turned around and waited for Sage.

Avaro balked. Dropping her head, she snorted at the ditch, which was easily four feet wide and two feet deep, then pawed the earth with her right front foot, dislodging chunks of dirt and small rocks.

"Come on, girl," Sage soothed, increasing the pressure of her calves. "You can do it."

Avaro disagreed and tried backing. Not an easy feat with her head considerably lower than her hind quarters.

"No, no." Sage prodded her forward to the edge and clucked her tongue.

All at once, Avaro launched herself in the air and popped over the ditch. As she hit the other side, she stumbled and nearly went down. Sage hung on. Barely. For several seconds, her surroundings were a blur. Then, thankfully, everything righted itself.

"You okay?" Gavin was on the ground, hurrying toward her, his horse's reins hanging loose.

"Yeah. I'm fine." She didn't mention her heart, which was beating a hundred miles an hour. "How's Avaro?"

The mare's legs trembled violently. It could be aftershock. Or worse. For all their great size, horses were delicate creatures and easily injured.

"See if she'll walk," Gavin instructed.

Sage gave Avaro her head. The mare obediently took one step. When it came to putting her other foot down, she resisted. Worried, Sage climbed off. Gavin was already beside the horse, squatting down to examine the suspect leg.

Sage stood behind him, watching over his shoulder as he ran his hand over Avaro's knee and down to her fetlock. When he finished, he stood and lifted her hoof, examining the underside.

"What do you think?" Sage asked.

"Hard to tell. I don't see a rock stuck in her shoe, and she doesn't appear to have any tenderness. Could just be residual pain. She landed pretty hard."

"Tell me about it." Sage was feeling her own residual pain.

"See if she'll walk now." Gavin straightened.

And just like that, they were as close as they'd been when they kissed earlier.

Gavin was thinking the same thing, Sage could see it in his eyes.

Funny, after all her talk about maintaining a strictly professional relationship, what she wanted most to do was press her lips to that very stubborn, very delectable mouth of his.

She bolstered her resolve...for all the good it did her. Avaro rubbed her head against Sage's arm, momentarily unbalancing her. Gavin came to her rescue by placing a hand on her shoulder and steadying her.

He had great hands. Strong, yet gentle. Sensitive and confident. Whether he was checking a horse for injuries or leading her away from a potentially awkward situation with Dan.

"Steady now," he murmured.

"I'm, uh, good. F-fine, really." Stammering? She didn't stammer.

"You sure?"

All right, already, her mind screamed. *Either kiss me or let me go.*

Making the choice for him, she lifted her face and raised her arms.

Gavin abruptly stepped back, his hand falling to his side.

Sage's cheeks burned. She covered her blunder by mounting Avaro. "Come on, girl."

Gavin also mounted, though he didn't immediately move or speak.

She was about to make a snappy comment, one she hoped

would cover her embarrassment at being rejected after practically throwing herself at him, when she followed Gavin's gaze to a trio of riders approaching from the opposite direction.

Avaro stared at them, ready to spring into action, every muscle in her body tense.

Gavin also stared. And there was no mistaking the ice-cold fury blazing in his eyes.

"EVENING," THE MAN IN THE LEAD said, a congenial smile on his face. "You folks having a problem?"

Gavin didn't respond.

The man halted in the middle of the trail, as did his two companions riding behind him. "Can we help?"

"You've already helped enough," Gavin ground out.

Sage didn't understand what was going on but recognized an insult when she heard one. Whoever this man was, Gavin disliked him intensely, though the feeling didn't appear to be mutual. That, or the man was considerably more adept at masking his baser emotions.

"How you doing, Gavin?" one of the young cowboys asked.

The other one tugged on the brim of his hat. "Gavin." His gaze fell on Sage. "Ma'am."

So, they all knew each other. Interesting.

Sage studied the one in front. He was probably around her age, his companions a few years younger. He was also handsome, wore clothes a cut above the rest and rode an exceptionally fine-looking gelding.

"My horse stumbled," she informed him, curious to see how this chance meeting would play out.

"Is she all right?"

"Appears to be."

"Isn't this the night of your monthly trail ride?" the man asked Gavin. "Where's the rest of your group?"

Rather than answer, Gavin said, "I'm surprised to find you here. As I recall, you don't much like being out in these mountains after dark."

The man smiled.

There was little room on the narrow trail. As a result, they stood facing each other, the three newcomers on one side, Gavin and Sage on the other. In order for them to pass, someone was going to have to move. From the rock hard set of Gavin's jaw, she doubted it would be him.

"We've been tracking that wild horse."

"Stay away from him." Gavin's voice took on a lethal edge. "He's mine."

The man rubbed the back of his neck, the casual movement tipping his hat forward. "Unless you can prove ownership, I don't believe there's any law saying I can't go after him."

"There is," Sage spoke up. "Only agents of the BLM can capture feral equine. If you *do* go after that horse on your own, you're breaking the law."

"No fooling?" The man's smile stretched wider as he apprised her from his higher vantage point. "How do you know that?"

"I'm Sage Navarre, a field agent with the Bureau of Land Management."

"Nicely played, Gavin." He chuckled with obvious good humor. "Did I say we were tracking a horse? I meant stray calves."

"Kind of late for that, isn't it?" Gavin asked with unmistakable challenge. "Calves are hard to spot in the dark."

"You're right." He regarded his companions. "How 'bout it, boys? Ready to head back?"

"Whatever you say, boss."

He inclined his head at Sage. "Good night, Ms. Navarre. It was a pleasure." The amused light in his eyes dimmed when he looked at Gavin, and his expression became almost sad.

"Give my regards to your father. And your sister the next time you talk to her. I hope they're both doing well."

"They are, no thanks to you."

The man simply nodded.

"'Night, Gavin," the second cowboy said. "Ma'am."

With a wave, all three men turned their horses around and headed back up the trail the way they'd come.

For several moments, Gavin didn't move.

"I think I can ride now." Sage waited a full minute, then attempted to break the silence again. "Or, we can stand here all night if you prefer."

Gavin busied himself checking his saddlebags.

"I know it's none of my business," she went on conversationally, "but he seemed nice. And genuinely concerned about your dad and sister."

Another minute of silence passed.

Sage grew impatient and expelled a long breath. "It's pretty clear you have some history with him—"

"That was Clay Duvall."

Something about the name rang a bell. Try as she might, she couldn't place it.

Gavin urged Shasta into a walk. Without looking back at her, he said, "His father's the one responsible for my family losing their land."

Ah, yes. That would explain the animosity.

"The SOB used the proceeds from the sale to build a rodeo arena, and now he's making money hand over fist."

Sage said nothing, for there was nothing *to* say.

Neither did Gavin, which made the ride back to the ranch incredibly long and tense.

GAVIN STOOD AT THE KITCHEN sink, staring out the window and sipping his coffee. The first gray streaks of dawn were just appearing in the eastern edge of what promised to be a clear, cloudless sky. A breeze rolled off the mountains, the mild gusts catching tree tops and teasing the branches. It was going to be another beautiful fall day.

Maybe it was also going to be a lucky day, and they'd find the mustang in the box canyon.

He still hadn't gotten over the shock of running into Clay Duvall last night on the trail and discovering he was also tracking the horse. Good thing Sage had been there and warned him off. If not, Gavin might have lost his composure and done something stupid. Again. He and Duvall had tangled before. Verbally and physically.

Gavin inherited his temper from his grandfather, as well as his penchant for staring out the kitchen window and a fondness for strong coffee. Not that his grandfather could brew a decent pot to save his life. Gavin wasn't much better. Nor was Ethan. Their father, on the other hand, could outcook most people. If not for him, they'd probably starve.

Draining the last swallow, Gavin surveyed the empty kitchen. He was usually the first one up, with Ethan a close second. Cassie woke next, on the days she didn't have school, and his father last, crawling out of bed just in time to fix everyone breakfast before they headed off in their different directions.

Hearing footsteps, he looked up, expecting to see his brother.

"Morning, son."

"Hey, Dad." Gavin rinsed his empty mug and set it in the dish rack to dry. "Trouble sleeping?" His father frequently suffered from insomnia, a side effect of his chronic depression according to the doctor.

"No. In fact, now that I think about it, I slept straight through the night."

That was a change. As was the smile on his father's face.

Granted, it wasn't much of a smile, but the first real one Gavin had noticed in a while.

"Coffee?" he asked, and reached in the cupboard for a clean mug.

"Half a cup. I need to cut back on my caffeine."

"Since when?"

"I'm not young anymore. Need to take care of my health if I expect to outlive you."

Had his father just made a joke?

Gavin passed him the mug, half-full as requested. "I thought Ethan would be up by now."

"He got home pretty late. I suspect he's sleeping in."

"You have any idea where he's going lately?" Gavin slid a chair out from under the table and sat beside his dad.

"The obvious answer would be a woman."

"Except you don't think so."

"My guess is he's breaking horses."

"Why won't he say anything?"

"He's afraid of failing."

Gavin mulled that over a bit. "Who do you suppose he's breaking horses for?" Powell Ranch wasn't the only one to succumb to progress or economic hardships in recent years.

"Clive Curtis maybe?"

That would explain the late hours. The Curtises lived twenty miles southeast of Mustang Valley.

Gavin would have liked to continue the conversation with his father but Cassie chose that moment to stumble into the kitchen, Blue tucked under her arm. He'd given up telling her she couldn't let the puppy sleep with her.

"Morning, honey," he said. "You're up early, too."

Seemed everyone except him was on a different schedule today.

"Hi, Dad. Hi, Grandpa." She gave each of them a quick,

one-armed hug en route to the refrigerator where she poured herself some orange juice.

Another surprise. Cassie didn't voluntarily dispense hugs.

An unexpected pressure pushed against the inside of Gavin's chest. It was, he realized after a moment, contentment. For the first time in a very long time he experienced a sense of family and with it, a rightness with the world.

Capturing the mustang and launching his stud and breeding business suddenly took on a whole new importance because this feeling wasn't something he wanted to lose. Ever.

"You don't mind watching Isa this afternoon, do you?" he asked Cassie.

"Can we go riding?"

Remembering the girls' request to go on the mustang roundup with him and Sage, he answered, "No farther than the pasture."

"Of course, Dad." She gave him a pained expression.

"I appreciate it. And so does Isa, I'm sure."

"She's a cool kid."

"She's not the only one." He smiled at his daughter.

She returned it, tentatively. But, like her grandfather earlier, it was genuine and directed straight at Gavin. The pressure against his chest grew heavier, squeezing his heart.

Or, was it the other way around? Had his heart suddenly grown bigger?

"I'll keep an eye on them, too," his dad offered. "You think you and Isa would like to go to that new ice cream parlor in town?"

"Seriously?"

"Seriously," her grandfather replied, his glance cutting to Gavin, his eyebrows raised in question.

"I'm told the Pralines and Cream is really good. Why don't you bring a gallon back with you?"

Cassie lifted Blue out in front of her, his hind legs dangling, and gave the puppy's nose a kiss. "You hear that, Blue? We're going to the ice cream parlor."

"He has to stay in the truck," Gavin's dad warned.

She responded with another pained expression.

A loud, impatient knock on the back door interrupted them.

Gavin got to his feet. "Probably Conner," he said, assuming their buddy had arrived early.

Way early, he thought, glancing at his watch.

Except it wasn't Conner at the door. Instead, Javier waited, his expression a mixture of excitement and worry.

"Señor Powell." Javier spoke only broken English and was sometimes difficult to understand. For a while, when he first came to work for the Powells, he'd lived in the old bunkhouse next to the barn. "Hurry. It is the horse."

Gavin reached for his jacket on the coatrack beside the door. "Which one?"

Perhaps one of the broodmares had delivered early, or a customer's horse injured itself. Mishaps and accidents weren't uncommon where animals were concerned.

"*El caballo salvaje.*" Javier made a motion with his hand for Gavin to hurry. "You must come now."

"The mustang?"

"*Sí.* He is here."

Gavin fumbled with his jacket zipper.

"Where?" His father had risen from the table to stand beside Gavin. Cassie was with him.

"The pasture. With the mama horses."

The mustang was on the ranch!

"Get Ethan," Gavin told his father, then raced after Javier.

Maybe they didn't have to go to the box canyon today.

Maybe, by some miracle, they could capture the mustang right here on the ranch.

He and Javier reached the outskirts of the pasture in mere minutes. Gavin slowed from a dead run to a jog, then to a complete stop. His breath, which had been coming fast and furious, was completely swept away. There, not thirty yards away in front of them, was the mustang. Standing motionless, black head held high in the air, his stance fearless, he confronted the intruders. Then, as if deciding they were of no great importance, he pranced in a circle, only to stop and arch his neck, his ears pricked forward.

"He's incredible."

"*Sí,*" Javier agreed, his tone reverent.

Gavin remembered reading long ago in high school that the ancient Greeks believed Poseidon gave man the horse. There had been a photograph in the text book of a marble statue by a famous sculptor. Gavin remembered little about the myth. But he did remember the stature of the horse, with its regal head, small yet powerful build and flowing mane and tail that resembled tongues of exploding fire.

He thought if Poseidon had indeed given man the horse, that first one must have looked something like his mustang.

Trotting back and forth in front of his audience, both the equine and human ones, the horse shook his head as if to draw attention to himself.

"I'll be damned," Ethan said, appearing beside Gavin, jacketless and his shirt only half-buttoned.

"*Sí,*" Javier repeated.

The broodmares, along with Avaro and old Chico, had congregated at the end of the pasture. The mares huddled a safe distance away, old Chico nearby. Avaro, on the other hand, alternately pressed against the fence, the rails cutting into her chest, or reversed her position and presented her backside to the mustang.

He reared, twisted the upper half of his body, and whinnied.

"I can't believe he ventured this close." Ethan tucked his loose shirttails into his jeans.

"Avaro's in heat." Gavin observed the courtship ritual with keen interest.

Ethan did, too. "I'd say he's in love and that it's mutual."

The mustang kicked up his hind legs, warning everyone else to stay away from his prize.

At the sound of approaching footsteps, Gavin looked over his shoulder. His father and Cassie hurried toward them, their eyes wide with astonishment.

"Oh, my gosh!" Cassie drew up beside Gavin and clutched his hand in both of hers. She hadn't done that since she was three.

He only this moment realized how much he'd missed it.

"You think the two of us can manage to surround and rope him?" he asked Ethan.

"I don't know. Lots of space out there."

"We should try."

"Hell, yes. Can't let an opportunity like this pass."

"I'm not thinking he'll cooperate."

Ethan chuckled. "You'd be disappointed if he did."

"We'd better hurry. I don't care how much in love he is, he's not going to stick around for long."

They no sooner started for the stables when Javier shouted, "The horse. Look!"

Gavin turned, afraid the mustang had run off. What he saw was the last thing he'd expected—Avaro sailing over the fence to join the mustang, her front legs tucked tight beneath her body.

All five of them stared, slack jawed.

"Who'd've thought it?" Ethan finally muttered.

Gavin remembered how high the mare had jumped when

she popped over the ditch yesterday and Sage's warning that she was an escape artist. "Dammit. I should have seen this coming."

"Don't blame yourself," Ethan said philosophically. "You had no way of knowing."

The two horses, united at last, galloped off toward the mountains, quickly shrinking to matching specks on the distant rise.

"We'd better saddle up and go after them. I'll call Conner. Tell him to get here fast."

"What about Sage?" Ethan asked. "You going to call her, too?"

Gavin could. He still had the business card she'd left with him that first day. "I will. Later. She has an appointment this morning."

"This is pretty important."

So was the paternity test, and she didn't need any distractions. Especially when there was nothing she could do.

"Let's ride out first. Follow their tracks. Avaro may have once been wild but not for the past three years. Chances are good she won't go far. She may even come back on her own after she and the mustang..." He glanced at Cassie. His daughter probably figured out what was going on. Nonetheless, Gavin wasn't ready to talk "sex" in front of her. "After a while," he finished.

"Should we cancel classes today?" Ethan asked.

"I'll cover you," their father volunteered. "Javier can handle the trail rides, if there are any."

Wayne Powell was a decent horseman, or had been at one time, and was certainly capable of instructing the beginner and intermediate students. It was just that he hadn't shown any interest in riding for years.

"You sure?" Gavin asked, uncertain how many more shocks he could take in one day.

"Cassie can help."

"And Isa, too," she piped up, excited at being included.

"You don't really think Avaro will come back on her own, do you?" Ethan remarked while he and Gavin were saddling up.

"It's possible."

Gavin was grasping at straws. But the alternative was telling Sage her horse had disappeared, and he was hoping like hell to avoid that.

Chapter Ten

While not exactly shabby, the testing facility was far from state-of-the-art. Sage had been expecting something along the lines of an urgent care clinic. Instead, the facility was four storefronts down from a chain grocery store, had darkly tinted windows and a sign out front advertising Walk-ins Welcome.

She'd phoned Roberto the moment she'd seen the place, sitting in her parked truck and staring at the tinted windows. He'd assured her that, besides being the closest testing facility to Mustang Valley, it came highly recommended.

Once inside, Sage had to admit the staff treated her and Isa professionally and tried to make both the chain of custody documentation process and the testing procedure itself as painless as possible. Her only complaint was having to wait… and wait…for the clerk to finish with the three people ahead of them, for a room to become available, for the technician who conducted the test.

Sage had pulled Isa close to her in each room they were asked to "Have a seat." She did it in part because the thermostat was set at a temperature suitable for penguins and in part because Isa was nervous. Sage even more so, though she had no reason to be.

The test was simply a nuisance. A hoop to jump through. In her overactive imagination, however, she envisioned ridiculous, impossible scenarios, ones where the test came back negative and she was insisting to Dan that some terrible mistake had been made.

Finally, they were done. Sage watched the technician package her and Isa's swabs and affix the labels.

"You should have the results in two to three business days," the technician told them. "After the other party comes in."

"Do you know when that will be?"

The man smiled patiently. "Couldn't tell you."

Of course not. She wasn't sure why she'd even asked.

After thanking him, Sage and Isa left the room and traveled the long hall. Pushing open the door to the reception area, she held it for Isa—who walked straight into Dan.

"Oh!" Sage automatically reached for her daughter, and the two of them took a step back. "You're here," she sputtered.

He glowered at them. "Have you finished with the test?"

"Yes." Why hadn't she asked him when he was coming? Then they could have avoided this…inconvenience.

"I saw you at the ranch," Isa said, her head tilted back to peer at him.

Dan ignored her in favor of Sage. "We need to talk."

She fumed. Not *"Can* I talk to you?" or "Do you have a minute?" No, he'd issued the order as if her sole option was to obey.

Worse, he'd snubbed Isa. His own daughter. For the second time.

"Come on." He began walking to the other side of the reception area where no one sat. When Sage didn't immediately follow, he glared at her and repeated irritably. "Come on."

Anger built inside her. She wanted nothing more than to tell Isa, "This rude and selfish man is your father, and you should be glad he wants nothing to do with you." Next, she'd lead Isa out the front door, never to see the bastard again.

Except this wasn't the time or place. Reluctantly, she sat

Isa in one of the chairs with a magazine, told her to wait and joined Dan.

"What is it?" she asked, purposefully infusing weary irritation in her voice.

A young woman sat across the waiting area, cradling a baby in her lap. She made no effort to hide the fact she was straining to hear Sage and Dan's conversation.

Sage fought for composure.

"I don't want you hanging around Powell Ranch," he said.

"I've been assigned to round up the mustang. I *have* to hang around Powell Ranch."

"But you don't have to go on trail rides."

Understanding dawned. He didn't want her mixing with his clients, word spreading that he had a daughter, one he didn't acknowledge or support. Bad for business and his image.

In that moment, she despised him. More than she'd thought possible.

"You have no say over what I do or where I go."

"This is a tricky situation, Sage."

"Cough up the money and Isa and I will be gone in a flash."

"I don't have it." His face reddened, from anger or embarrassment or frustration, she couldn't tell.

"I find that hard to believe, Dan. You live in a nice house, drive a new truck and seem to have plenty of clients."

She caught a glimpse of Isa, sitting with the unopened magazine in her lap and watching them with unblinking eyes. Sage's heart constricted. Her little girl didn't deserve this.

Reining in her temper, she vowed to stick to her original plan. No scenes.

"I won't give up, Dan. Not until you pay the child support."

"My disposable income is currently tied up in other ventures," he said.

"Other ventures?"

"The Powells, for one. Horses, for another."

"I don't care where your money is. Isa and I have been more than patient and aren't waiting any longer."

"You have no choice."

She stared at him, hardly recognizing the man before her. "What happened, Dan? You used to adore Isa."

An undefinable emotion flickered in his eyes.

All at once, she knew. Something she should have figured out long ago. "It's your wife."

"What are you talking about?"

"You met her while we were still together."

"Big deal. We weren't involved."

"Liar. That's why you're insisting on the paternity test. You think I could have been unfaithful because you were."

"Don't go there, Sage," he growled.

Too late. She'd already gone. And the guilt written all over his face proved she'd uncovered his dirty secret.

"On second thought, I'm glad Isa won't ever know you."

Turning her back on him, she went to her daughter—*hers,* not theirs—and held out a hand. Isa took it, her sweet face marred by confusion and nervousness.

"Is he my daddy?" she whispered, casting a furtive glance at Dan.

"We'll talk outside, *mija.*"

As they approached the door, it swung opened.

Dan's pregnant wife stood on the other side, their little boy in tow.

Both she and Sage came to an abrupt halt, their gazes assessing each other and the children at their sides. Judging by the other woman's look of disdain, Sage and Isa came up short.

Sage refused to step aside. Petty, but she didn't care. As a result, Dan's wife had no choice but to skirt around them. She did so, giving them a wide, wide berth.

The feeling's mutual, Sage thought.

Telling herself it would be worth it in the end, she trudged out the door and to the parking lot.

If only she didn't have to go back to the ranch today, she'd take Isa somewhere fun. They could forget all about this morning. But she did have to go back. For the mustang. The same mustang Gavin would use in his stud and breeding business. The business where Dan's money was supposedly tied up.

The irony of the situation didn't escape her. By doing her job, helping Gavin, she was actually hurting Isa's chances of recovering the money Dan owed.

Opening the passenger side door, she helped Isa into the truck and buckled her seat belt.

"Who was that lady and little boy?" she asked. "Is he my brother?"

Sometimes, like right now, Sage wished Isa wasn't so smart for her age. She'd have to explain. Isa was entitled to the truth. At least, a simplified version.

"I saw a park up the road with some swings and picnic tables. Why don't we go there and Mama will tell you everything. Okay?"

GAVIN, ETHAN AND CONNER had just returned from searching for Avaro when Sage pulled into the ranch. He wished he had something better to tell her. Unfortunately, they not only hadn't found her horse, they lost the tracks a mile into the mountains.

With school on fall break, there were more than the usual number of people for a Monday, many of them kids. Maybe because of that, and the fact he was distracted by the morning's events, he hadn't noticed Cassie right away as he walked from the stables. Why would he? She didn't hang around with the kids who came to the ranch. She didn't hang around with anyone her age.

Until today, apparently.

A group of middle school students, mostly girls, were playing some sort of game in the open area in front of the arena. Cassie was smack-dab in the center, participating. And laughing. Blue nipped at her heels as she ran, then spun and shrieked gleefully when another girl grabbed the back of her shirt.

It was a sight Gavin had only dreamed of seeing.

He committed it to memory for the next time Cassie's mother asked how their daughter was doing.

Isa fled Sage's truck the moment it was parked and ran straight for Cassie. Reaching her, the little girl flung her arms around Cassie's waist and clung to her as if they'd been separated for years instead of hours. Cassie gave Isa's back a comforting pat, much like the ones Gavin had given her when she was young. He couldn't hear what the two were saying, but he suspected whatever Cassie uttered was the right thing, for Isa slowly extracted herself and smiled...through her tears.

She'd been crying.

Hearing footsteps behind him, Gavin turned around to see Sage approaching. By the expression she wore, she'd also been through an emotional wringer, though her eyes were dry. He assumed the paternity test hadn't gone well or had been a lot tougher than she'd anticipated.

"Hey," he said when she approached.

"Hi."

He went to her and cupped her cheek in his palm, stroking her smooth skin with the pad of his thumb. Ethan had already figured out there was something between Gavin and Sage. Who cared if anyone else figured it out, too?

She didn't pull away. Covering his hand with hers, she

leaned into him, tucking her head into the crook of his neck. Gavin's other arm came up and circled her protectively. She felt good nestled against him. More than good. She felt as though she'd been designed to fit precisely there, and he'd only been waiting for her to show up.

They stood like that for several moments. Gavin was glad he could give her what she needed. He also dreaded having to add to her troubles.

"You're a good man, Gavin Powell," she murmured, her warm breath caressing his exposed neck.

"No, I'm not. I've made a lot of mistakes in my life."

"Who hasn't? But you do the best you can."

"So do you."

"I wish I didn't have to involve you in my problems. I'd hate for there to be any...repercussions."

Gavin thought of Dan's warning phone call the previous night. "Did Dan say something to you?"

"He showed up at the testing facility just as we were leaving. Along with his wife and son."

"Was Isa there?"

"Yes. He was terrible to her."

That explained the tears. "I'm sorry, honey." When she didn't immediately respond, he asked. "What else?"

She sighed and withdrew.

He'd have preferred to continue holding her but it was impossible. "Sage?"

"He threatened me and, indirectly, your family if I didn't stay away from you and the ranch, other than going after the mustang."

Maybe holding each other out in the open wasn't such a good idea after all. Dan's clients were obviously feeding him information. Gavin and Sage would have to be more discreet in the future. But not stop. He had every intention of holding her again *and* kissing her.

"Don't worry about Dan," he said.

"I wish it was that easy. He won't back off."

"No, he won't. But right now, we have a slightly bigger problem."

"What's that?"

"Sage, I'm sorry." He swallowed before continuing. "Avaro escaped early this morning."

She didn't immediately speak. When she did, she struggled. "H-how? Was the f-fence...broken?"

"No. She jumped it. We've been out looking for her. Came back because we knew you were arriving soon."

"I don't understand." Her hand rested at the base of her throat. "We put her in with other horses so this wouldn't happen."

"The mustang was here."

"At the ranch!"

"Outside the pasture. That's when she jumped the fence. Javier, Ethan and I saw the whole thing. We were going to go after the mustang, try to rope him, but then Avaro escaped, and the two of them ran off. I didn't call you, I knew you had the paternity test. And I figured it was better that we went after her right away."

"We have to go back out," Sage said in a rush.

"As soon as we saddle up a horse for you and fresh ones for Ethan, Conner and I. Dad will keep an eye on the girls. He's also packing us a lunch and some drinks."

"Mama, look at Blue's new collar." Isa came running over, the puppy patiently coping with his bumpy ride. Cassie came, too. "He outgrew his other one already." Isa took one look at her mother and stopped suddenly. "What's wrong?"

"Avaro's missing," Sage told the girls. "We're leaving now to look for her."

"Can we come?" Cassie asked.

"That's not a good idea," Gavin said.

"Why not? The more people looking, the better the chance of finding her. Right?"

"We'll handle it, Cassie. You and Isa are going to stay here with Grandpa."

"Not fair." Her bottom lip protruded stubbornly.

Isa set the puppy on the ground, went over to Sage and hugged her. "Poor Mama."

Sage stroked the girl's hair. "You be good for Mr. Powell, promise?"

Isa nodded.

"How 'bout you head into the house," Gavin suggested. "Fix yourselves some lunch."

Sage kissed the top of Isa's head, then she and Gavin started toward the stables.

Cassie accompanied Isa, though storming off was probably a better description. Gavin put the incident from his mind. He'd make amends later.

At the moment, finding Avaro took precedence.

GAVIN PEERED THROUGH the binoculars, hoping to see a movement among the overgrown brush in the rocky ravine below. They'd been riding the Tom Thumb Trail for the past two hours, with no more luck than before.

"See anything?" Sage asked. She sat astride one of the ranch's more dependable horses, a gelding Ethan had broken to ride right before he joined the Marines.

"No," Gavin answered, and lowered the binoculars. "Nothing."

"Damn. Where could she be?"

About a million and one places, but Gavin didn't voice the thought aloud. Sage was already plenty worried.

"Let's keep going." He loosened his reins, the only cue his horse needed. The mare, an older sister of Shasta from the same original mustang lines, started up the trail, her head lowered, her powerful front legs digging into the steep and uneven ground.

They'd split into two groups for the afternoon search. Gavin and Sage in one, Ethan and Conner in the other. As well as looking for Avaro, Ethan and Conner were going to the box canyon to retrieve the mares. There was no point in leaving them another night. The mustang would not likely return now that he had Avaro.

Gavin's cell phone suddenly rang, startling him. Though far from any tower, he sometimes got reception in odd little pockets throughout the preserve. How good the reception was depended on the weather.

He reined in his horse and removed his phone from his pocket. His brother's name appeared on the display. Skipping any preamble, he answered brusquely, "Find her?"

"Not yet. What about you?"

"Nothing."

"How's Sage holding up?"

Though his back was to her, Gavin sensed her gaze on him. "Well enough."

"Conner and I are just getting ready to head over to the canyon."

"I think we'll check out the reservoir at the golf resort." It was a long shot, but worth investigating.

"I doubt my phone will work after this. I'll send up a flare if we spot the horses."

"I'll do the same."

Disconnecting, Gavin continued along the trail. Sage didn't ask about the call, the gist of which was probably obvious from listening to his end of the conversation. Not three minutes later, his phone rang again. Hoping it was Ethan with good news, Gavin was surprised to see his father's number appear on the display.

"Hey, Dad. Everything okay?"

"No, it's bad. The girls are missing."

Chapter Eleven

"Missing!" Panic ripped through Gavin.

"I've been searching for the last twenty minutes." Worry strained his father's voice. "The girls aren't anywhere on the ranch."

"Are they on horseback or foot?"

"Horseback. Javier said he saw them riding Chico and Barbie Doll along the back pasture about an hour ago."

"Why didn't he stop them?"

"He didn't know. It wasn't his job to watch the girls. It was mine." His father sounded desperate. "I screwed up. I lay down for a nap."

"A nap?" Gavin snapped, unable to help himself. His father had a habit of sleeping in the afternoon. But why today of all days? "Dammit, Dad."

Avaro escaping with the mustang paled in comparison to this crisis.

"What is it?" Sage had nudged her horse close to Gavin's. "Tell me," she insisted.

Gavin held the phone away from his mouth. "Cassie and Isa are apparently riding in the preserve. Alone."

"Apparently!"

"Javier saw them head out about an hour ago."

"And your dad was napping?" Her voice rose with growing agitation.

"We'll find them. Don't worry." He had to stay calm. Think clearly. "They couldn't have gotten far, and I know every inch of these mountains."

He did, it was true. But there were a lot of mountains in this range.

"Javier and I will saddle up right away," his father interrupted. "I'll alert Rebecca in case the girls come back."

"And I'll call Ethan. He and Conner are on their way to the box canyon." He tried to think of where Cassie might take Isa. "You and Javier ride the west ridge. The picnic site is one of Cassie's favorites places."

"Please tell Sage how sorry I am."

He glanced at her. She was leaning forward in the saddle, hanging on his every word.

"We'll worry about that later," he said. "Contact the sheriff's office before you and Javier leave. Report the girls missing."

Gavin and his father discussed several last details, then disconnected. Contacting Ethan next, Gavin filled in his brother with clipped, urgent sentences. They agreed he and Conner should continue onto the box canyon as that route ran south of the ranch. Between all three search parties, they'd have much of the preserve's northern section covered.

"If you find them, send up a flare," Gavin said. "I'll do the same."

He hesitated after disconnecting. There had to be more he could do, someone he could call to help beside the sheriff. They had friends in the area. People who would come to their aid. Unfortunately, time wasn't on their side. At most, ninety minutes of daylight remained.

He didn't want to think about how cold it got in these mountains at night.

"What possessed Cassie to take Isa on a ride?" Sage blinked back tears, fighting for composure.

Gavin didn't defend his daughter. She knew better, and there was no excuse for taking Isa with her. He recalled Cassie storming off to the house, angry she couldn't go with them to search for Avaro. He should have taken a moment to talk to her and explain.

"This isn't just Cassie's fault or my dad's. It's mine, too. But we can divvy up the blame later, after she and Isa are home."

"Does Cassie carry a cell phone?"

"She lost it last week, and I haven't replaced it yet. No reason. She hasn't been off the ranch, what with school on break."

Gavin cursed the lousy stroke of luck. Taking out his binoculars, he scanned the distant rises. It was unlikely he'd spot the girls from their position at the base of a large hill. Still, he tried.

"If I told Isa once, I told her a thousand times not to go anywhere without checking with me first." Sage rubbed her temple with trembling fingers. "This morning at the testing facility...she was so upset afterward. She might be acting out."

He reached over and grasped her hand. It was cold and clammy. Like his. "We're going to find them, honey. And they'll be just fine. I promise." He squeezed her fingers, hoping that the more pressure he applied, the more she'd believe him.

"Can we go now? Please."

He started to put his phone away, only to have it ring again. Thank God he had decent reception.

"It's Ethan." Heart hammering, he answered the call. "Yeah."

"I have an idea." Static on the line made it hard for Gavin to hear everything. "Extra manpower for the search."

"Tell me." He angled the phone in an attempt to improve the connection.

"Clay Duvall."

"Who?" Gavin heard his brother. He just thought he had to be mistaken.

"Duvall. He'll help us. And he has a half-dozen men working for him he can recruit."

Every nerve in Gavin's body screamed no. He didn't want to involve Duvall or have anything to do with the man. Not after his and his father's betrayal.

Except that Ethan was right. There was an unspoken code among the cowboys, times when differences were put aside. This was one of them. And Duvall would come through.

Swallowing his pride and resentment, which was far from easy, Gavin instructed his brother, "Call him."

"I already did. He and his men are on their way."

Leave it to Ethan to know the right thing to do.

"Have them check out the northwest rim first."

Gavin and Sage continued on the Tom Thumb Trail for another half hour. They encountered only two sets of hikers, neither of which had seen any other riders, much less two children on horseback. In between, Gavin and Sage didn't talk much. That left each of them to cope with their guilt and anxiety in silence.

On every rise that afforded them a decent view, they stopped. While Gavin glassed the area with his binoculars, Sage hollered for the girls. Her shaky voice carried, echoing off the sheer rock faces. There was no answer, not that Gavin expected one. He felt certain his father and Javier would locate the girls at the picnic site.

He hadn't yet decided on Cassie's punishment, his mind too filled with thoughts of finding her and Isa. His daughter would no doubt be unhappy with him. Resent him. And she would probably want to return to her mother at Christmastime, if not before.

At least she would be safe.

All at once, Gavin saw it. There, to their left, a tiny missile climbing skyward, a column of orange smoke trailing behind it. His relief was so strong, his chest hurt.

"Look!" he shouted.

"Thank God," Sage said from behind him, and burst into tears.

Noting the southern location of the flare, he pulled out his cell phone to call Ethan. The display registered no signal. He resisted the urge to fling the phone into the ravine below.

Instead, he said, "Let's hurry." They had less than an hour of daylight left.

"Where are they?" Sage asked as they pushed their horses for more speed up the steep hill.

"Near the box canyon." Five miles at least from the picnic site.

"Do you think they're all right?"

He refused to think Cassie and Isa might be in trouble or injured. "I'm sure they are."

Only, he wasn't.

"How long will it take us to get there?"

"Forty-five minutes if we haul ass."

It was the longest forty-five minutes of Gavin's life.

Too soon, the smoke from the flare dissipated, leaving him uncertain as to Ethan's exact location. Every ten minutes he tried to reach his brother. Always, the infuriating "no service" message flashed on his phone's display. When they got within a quarter mile of the entrance to the box canyon, he cupped his hands to his mouth and shouted his brother's name. No one answered.

Shit.

"Where are they?" Sage asked. She'd held herself together

well during their rough-and-tumble ride. But stress and exhaustion showed on her face and in the weary slump of her shoulders.

"They can't be far."

"Are you sure the flare was launched around here?"

"Positive."

A shrill whistle came from a ridge some two hundred yards to the east. Gavin swung around in the saddle and immediately identified the three riders.

"Who are they?" Sage asked.

"Clay Duvall and two of his men. They must have followed the flare, too."

Duvall waved from his position in front, and Gavin raised his hand in reply.

At that moment, another flare appeared in the sky, not more than a mile away by Gavin's estimation. He smiled for the first time all day. When he next saw his brother, he was going to give him a big kiss and not care who saw.

"Isn't that coming from inside the box canyon?" Sage stood in her stirrups, straining to see.

"The far end, I'd say." He could have kicked himself for not thinking of it earlier. "I bet the girls went after the mares and Ethan found them."

"Or after the *mustang*. They did ask to go with us."

He grumbled. "When I get hold of Cassie, I'm going to wring—"

"Hug her. You're going to hug her."

"Yes," Gavin conceded. "But rest assured, there will be a loss of privileges."

They hurried the remaining distance to the canyon with nightfall chasing them the entire way.

Ethan sat astride his horse about a quarter mile past the entrance.

"Where are they?" Gavin asked when he and Sage drew near.

"At the pen. They're okay."

Sage sighed.

"Is Conner with them?"

"He's over there." Ethan pointed to a spot fifty yards away.

Conner tipped his hat.

"Why isn't one of you with the girls?" Sage demanded.

"Because we found more than your two daughters." Ethan's grin stretched from ear to ear. "Your mare's tied up at the pen."

"Really!" Sage's anger vanished, replaced by surprise.

"And something else," Ethan said, grinning even wider.

Excitement exploded inside Gavin as the reason for his brother's exuberance hit him.

"The mustang's here."

Ethan chuckled. "Looks like we're having us a wild-horse roundup tonight."

SAGE HAD NEVER BEEN ON A HORSE roundup quite like this one. It wasn't just the lack of helicopters and manpower. The techniques the men used reminded her of another era altogether, when cowboys had only their ropes and their wits at their disposal.

Clay Duvall, the neighbor whom Gavin held a grudge against, had arrived with his two wranglers. So had Gavin's father and Javier.

Sage stayed with the girls and watched from their vantage point atop a rocky peak near the mares' pen. She would have rather been a part of the roundup but conceded she possessed neither the roping skills required, nor the experience. These eight men, even with their differences and dislike of each other, knew what to do without being told. They might have been on a hundred roundups together considering how well they worked as a team.

"Mama, I'm sorry," Isa apologized for the third time in a meek voice. She sat huddled beside Sage, hugging her drawn up knees.

"We'll talk later, *mija*." And they would. But for now, Sage wanted to watch the roundup. What she could see of it. Dusk had already fallen. Complete darkness wasn't far behind.

Gavin, Ethan, Conner and Clay Duvall circled the mustang on their horses, having driven him away from the mares and to the farthest corner of the canyon. The remaining men formed a second outer circle. Their job was to stop the mustang if he tried to escape—which he did, every few minutes.

Avaro whinnied from where she was tied to a branch, agitated by all the horses and activity.

"Watch out!" Cassie hollered.

The mustang had tried to cut between Gavin and Ethan in a frantic dash for freedom. They quickly stopped him by blocking his escape route. Frustrated, he galloped in a circle, head lowered and hind legs kicking.

"Why don't they catch him?" Isa asked.

"They're tiring him out so he won't fight so much and it'll be easier."

"How long will that take? I'm hungry."

Sage wanted to tell her daughter she should have thought of food before riding off with Cassie, but didn't.

The mustang was stubborn and determined. He was also outnumbered and fast becoming exhausted. Each attempt he made to break loose was immediately thwarted and further depleted his energy.

Minute by minute, foot by foot, the circle surrounding him closed. Suddenly, Ethan threw his rope at the mustang…and missed. Angry, the mustang let out a high-pitched squeal and ran in the opposite direction, only to be stopped by the men waiting there. Sage lost track of him after that. It was too dark to see more than thirty feet beyond where they sat.

"Heads-up," Gavin shouted. "He's coming your way."

In the next instant, the mustang materialized in front of Sage and the girls as if formed from thin air. He seemed as surprised to see them as they were him and pawed the ground menacingly.

Sage stared, her attention riveted. He was truly a magnificent sight, and her heart swelled with wonder.

"He's beautiful," Cassie whispered.

Sage started to rise, compelled by an emotion she couldn't define. It was as if the horse demanded she honor him with a show of respect.

The rope came from nowhere, sailing through the air to land squarely around the mustang's neck.

She barely had time to realize what was happening when another rope flew by, also hitting its mark.

The mustang summoned the last of his strength and fought his constraints. Thrusting his head from side to side, he reared, came down and reared again, his breathing labored.

Gavin leaped to the ground. His horse, trained in calf roping, slowly backed up, pulling the rope connected to his saddle horn taut.

Ethan also dismounted. As the remaining men on horseback closed the circle, he and Gavin approached the mustang.

"Easy, boy." Gavin spoke softly, his hand raised in front of him. "It's going to be all right."

The mustang didn't agree and bared his teeth.

"I'm not going to hurt you."

"Watch he doesn't bite you," Ethan warned.

Gavin stopped five feet in front of the horse. Sage sensed in him the same wonder she'd felt earlier. She thought for a moment he might dare approach the horse and lay a hand on him. He didn't, which turned out to be a smart move. The horse reared again, this time slicing the air with his front hooves.

"He likes you, bro," Ethan said with a chuckle.

"It's mutual." There was no humor in Gavin's voice, only admiration.

They stared at each other, he and the horse. And then something magical happened. The horse stopped fighting. Maybe he was tired. Or maybe he decided he'd met his match. Sage preferred to think the horse and man had come to some kind of understanding.

Gavin let out a long, satisfied breath. "What do you say we take him home?"

The trip back to the ranch was arduous. Isa became whiney and cranky halfway there. Probably due to hunger and fatigue and, possibly, fear of what punishment lay ahead of her. The mustang, with both ropes still tied around his neck, and Gavin and Ethan at the end of each one, refused to cooperate. Every step he took was only because he had no choice.

Sage had always assumed the horse was an escapee from either the Indian reservation or a nearby ranch. Seeing him now, his reaction to his captors, it was clear he'd had little or no human contact for a very long time, if ever.

Could he be, as Gavin believed, the last descendant of the wild mustangs that once roamed this area?

No, that was impossible. Right?

Conner, Javier and Gavin's dad brought up the rear, each of them leading a mare. Gavin's two horses carried the remaining equipment and supplies in their hastily loaded pack saddles. Clay Duvall and his wranglers had taken a different trail, one that would lead them back to his place. Before parting, Ethan had thanked his neighbor warmly and shook his hand. Gavin's father hadn't been quite so friendly, though his brief conversation with Clay Duvall was civil enough.

Not Gavin. His entire exchange with the other man consisted of a nod, and a terse one at that.

Eventually, the lights of Powell Ranch came into sight. Not long after, they reached the pasture fence.

"Where should we put him?" Ethan asked.

Gavin pondered their captive. "I'm thinking the round pen. It has the highest fence on the property."

A high fence would probably come in handy, considering what Avaro had done. And the mustang was far more determined to regain his freedom.

When they reached the stables, everyone dismounted. It was decided that Conner and Javier would unsaddle all the mounts and put them up for the night. The girls went with Gavin's dad into the house, assigned to helping him throw together a quick supper for everyone.

Getting the mustang into the round pen proved to be a process. With Gavin pulling him, and Ethan behind guarding his back, they managed to get him through the narrow gate after ten long and exhausting minutes. When they finally shut the gate, both men were sweating and Ethan was limping badly.

He rubbed his knee and grunted in pain. "I'm surprised he's got that much energy left after all we put him through."

"I'm not." Gavin stood at the fence.

The mustang put on a show, trotting back and forth and snorting with frustration. Every few seconds, he would stop and glare angrily at Gavin.

Sage went to stand beside him. "He won't be easy to tame. You have your work cut out for you."

Gavin smiled with pleasure.

Conner carried over the galvanized steel tub they'd brought back from the canyon. He pushed it under the bottom railing of the round pen. Uncoiling a nearby hose, he filled the tub with water. From a safe place on the opposite side of the pen, the mustang eyed the hose as if it were a poisonous snake.

Sage knew from BLM roundups that feral horses seldom drank right away. "By morning," she said, "he'll be thirsty."

Javier came, too, bringing a thick flake of hay which he pushed under the bottom railing next to the tub.

The mustang stretched his head forward, his nostrils flaring, but he didn't move from his spot. No worries. He would also eat by morning, if not sooner.

"How old do you think he is?" Sage asked.

"Hard to say without a closer inspection. But my guess is he's young. Three. Five, maybe."

Sage thought so, too.

When Gavin's dad rang the dinner bell fifteen minutes later, everyone was still standing at the railing, transfixed. The mustang had yet to move from his spot.

"I don't know about you guys, but I'm hungry." Ethan clapped Conner on the back. "You, too, Javier." He dragged the smaller man along. "Eat with us."

The three of them strolled to the house, continuing their loud and lively conversation.

Gavin was slow to move.

"Come on." Sage rested a hand on his shoulder. Like everyone else, she was feeling happy. For a day that had started out awful, it had certainly ended on a high note. "We've got some celebrating to do."

"We do." He turned toward her. "And I want to start now."

His ice-blue eyes, so dark in the moonlight, swept over her face. She had only seconds to prepare before his arm circled her waist, and he drew her flush against him.

A small gasp escaped her, not of protest but delight—at his actions and her reaction to them. Her instincts told her this kiss would be nothing like their previous one…and infinitely more exciting.

Her instincts weren't wrong.

Even before his mouth came rushing down to claim hers, she tensed in eager anticipation. For an instant, when his lips first met hers, she thought her feet had truly left the ground.

The impracticality of any romance developing between them became a distant, insignificant concern as his arms secured her more snugly to him and his tongue sought entry. She opened herself to him, sighing softly as he explored her mouth, melting inside and out as the kiss went on and on.

He was incredibly skilled, demanding but also giving. Oh, yes, giving. The effects of his generosity cascaded through her, lighting tiny sparks at each nerve ending. She could, and did, lose herself. In his masculine scent. In the feel of his muscles bunching beneath her fingers. In the caress of his breath on her cheek as he broke off the kiss, groaned, then returned for more.

Good, because she wasn't ready to stop, either.

He angled her sideway and the next thing she knew, he'd pinned her between him and the round pen. His hands, large and strong, cradled her face, their callused palms stroking her cheeks with a gentleness that touched her as much as it excited her.

The mustang, undoubtedly confused at what his human captors were doing, snorted angrily and pawed the ground.

Gavin slowed the tempo of their kiss but didn't stop.

"Dad! Sage!" Cassie's voice carried from the house. It was followed by more ringing of the dinner bell. "Hurry. We're hungry."

Gavin slid his mouth from Sage's, only to tickle her earlobe with his lips and teeth.

"We'd better go," she murmured, as reluctant as him for the moment to end.

He closed his eyes, collected himself and stepped back.

She moved from the railing on legs a little unsteady, gave the mustang one last look and started toward the house.

An acute awkwardness settled over them—only until Gavin took hold of her hand and linked their fingers.

Sage supposed they had a lot to talk about. It was very unlikely their relationship would go anywhere. Even if she resolved her differences with Dan, she and Isa were leaving in a matter of days.

Suddenly the prospect of going home to Show Low didn't hold nearly the same appeal as it had this morning.

Chapter Twelve

"Can we stand next to the pen?" the reporter asked.

"I don't think that would be a good idea." Gavin pushed his cowboy hat back and scratched his forehead thoughtfully.

"Why not?"

"He got mad at the last reporter and bit him on the…right cheek."

"Cheek as in…" The reporter grimaced.

"Yeah, that one," Gavin confirmed.

The woman camera operator giggled, then sobered when the reporter glowered at her.

"How about we stand over here?" The reporter relocated a respectable distance away from the pen. "Sal, can you get a shot of the horse in the background?"

"No problem."

Gavin was happy to oblige them. Given his choice, he'd rather the mustang not be filmed up close. Part of him worried that someone would recognize the horse and come forward, claiming ownership.

He still had no idea who'd leaked the story to the news media or why, though his suspicions were leaning toward Conner. He certainly understood the interest. It wasn't every day a horse was found roaming an urban preserve. There was also his family's long-standing ties to the valley, and that the horse was captured as a result of searching for two lost girls.

"Are your daughters here?" the reporter asked as the camera operator positioned them according to the best light. "I'd like to interview them, too."

"Only one of the girls is mine. And she's not here now."

Gavin's father had taken Cassie with him to Scottsdale for a dentist appointment. After that, they were running errands, which included the bank, the post office and, lastly, the warehouse food store. They'd be gone for the rest of the afternoon. Cassie despised their monthly stock-up shopping trips. She despised the unpacking of everything they brought home even more. Accompanying her grandfather was part of her punishment for taking off without permission or telling anyone about it and, Gavin thought, a fitting one.

Cassie had tried her best to sweet-talk him out of it, saying if she and Isa hadn't gone in search of the mustang, they'd have never found him. The argument got her nowhere. Funny thing was, she hadn't been all that mad at Gavin. Once she realized there was no swaying him, she backed off.

He wasn't sure he'd ever understand the twelve-year-old female mind.

"The other girl," Gavin continued, "is the daughter of…" He hesitated, not sure what to call Sage. After their fiery kiss last night, he didn't think of her as just the BLM agent who'd come to Mustang Valley to assist with rounding up the horse.

That was, however, what he told the reporter. The man, the whole world, didn't need to know about Gavin and Sage's relationship. Not yet. Certainly not until they'd figured it out themselves. Besides, if Dan got wind of their involvement, no telling how he'd react.

"Who else went with you on the roundup?" the reporter asked.

"My brother, a buddy of ours and…" Again Gavin hesitated. "Some neighbors."

He appreciated Clay Duvall's help. However, he was nowhere ready to bury the hatchet. Bud Duvall had ruined the Powells' lives, and Clay had profited every bit as much as his father from the sale of their land.

The reporter continued to fire questions at Gavin about the mustang. He answered, squinting into the early afternoon sun. He didn't much like being interviewed and would have refused under different circumstances. Except his phone hadn't stopped ringing all day. And the callers weren't just reporters or folks curious about the mustang. Many were potential new customers interested in taking lessons or boarding their horse. After the first TV news segment ran on the midday edition, people started inquiring about breeding their horses to the mustang.

Gavin couldn't believe it. If only a percentage of the callers became actual customers, the increase in revenues would be enough to make a difference in his family's lives, if not change them completely.

It would take time. Nothing happened overnight. He might even be able to buy Dan out eventually.

The idea appealed to him on many levels.

So, for those reasons and others, he tolerated the various reporters and patiently answered the same questions again and again.

Ethan sauntered over during the interview, a wide grin splitting his face. He was enjoying the attention they were receiving considerably more than Gavin.

Distracted, Gavin tripped over his next sentence.

The reporter told the camera operator to cut and glanced backward. "Is that your brother?"

"Yes."

"Mr. Powell!" The reporter gestured at Ethan. "Mind if we interview you, too?"

"Naw, that's all right."

"I'm sure our viewers would enjoy hearing about how a man with only one leg manages to work as a cowboy."

How did the reporter know that? Gavin hadn't mentioned it. Damn Conner, if indeed it was him.

Ethan's grin dissolved. "My brother's the one in charge of the ranch and the mustang. It's him you need to talk to."

He walked away, leaving the reporter confused and irritated.

The interview progressed poorly after that. Gavin's cell phone ringing twice didn't help. While the reporter and camera operator were getting into their van, Ethan's red Dodge truck rumbled past.

Gavin's irritation spiked. Fine, the reporter had been a jerk, but this wasn't a good day for Ethan to be playing hooky. They were far too busy.

Gavin's cell phone rang yet again. As he spoke to the potential new customer, reciting boarding rates and lesson fees, Sage arrived. He forgot all about his caller as memories of their kiss filled his mind.

She drove behind the barn to park. He walked over, meeting her halfway. He noticed she carried a briefcase.

"You here on business?" he asked, half joking.

"As a matter of fact—" she smiled brightly "—I am."

He was tempted to take her in his arms. Common sense prevailed.

"My supervisor wants me to email him pictures of the horse. And I brought some paperwork for you to complete in order to start the adoption process."

"Great." They headed toward the round pen and the mustang. "Where's Isa?"

"Not coming today. I felt she needed a couple days away from the ranch and Chico to help drive the lesson home."

"I bet she's taking that hard."

"Very."

"You will bring her back." Gavin stopped himself from adding, *before you leave*. He didn't want to think about Sage returning to Show Low.

"Yes, of course." she glanced at the arena and stables. "Where is everyone?"

By *everyone*, Gavin knew she meant his family. The ranch was crowded today and not just because of the reporters. All the regulars also wanted a peek at the mustang. He'd had to station Javier near the round pen in order to run interference.

"Dad took Cassie into Scottsdale. Ethan left right before you arrived. I have no idea when any of them will be back."

At the round pen, the mustang greeted him and Sage the same way he did everyone else—by lowering his head, snorting and backing himself into the farthest corner.

Sage set her briefcase on the ground, opened it and removed a digital camera. "Have you thought of a name for him yet?"

"No. Been too busy."

"It needs to be something really special." She stood on the bottom rung and powered up the camera. At the small noise, the mustang raised his head, his ears pricked forward, and stared intently at them. "Would you look at that. Am I wrong, or is he posing?"

Gavin laughed. "Who'd have guessed he's a ham?"

Three pictures later, the mustang had enough. He trotted back and forth in the pen, a shower of soft dirt exploding from beneath his feet. Sage continued taking pictures until she had at least two dozen. Stepping down from the railing, she reviewed the pictures, sharing them with Gavin.

Heads bent close together, they commented on each shot.

It was hard for Gavin not to lean in and steal a kiss from her. She must have sensed his thoughts, or was having similar ones herself, for she tilted her head to gaze at him, invitation in her eyes.

Oh, hell, Gavin thought, *why not?* Who cared about propriety?

He reached for her—only to be distracted by a vehicle roaring to a dirt-spitting stop not far from them. He glanced up to see who it was with the lousy timing and cursed under his breath.

Dan Rivera pushed open his truck door and emerged, his booted feet hitting the ground with purpose.

Beside him, Sage stiffened.

"It's all right," Gavin murmured. "He didn't see anything except us looking at the pictures you took."

Not entirely true but a plausible excuse if Dan should question them.

He didn't and marched toward them, scowling at Sage.

Gavin had been expecting Dan. He'd called his partner last night to give him the good news. Dan had said he'd be over later in the day. Too bad later in the day coincided with the exact moment Gavin had decided to kiss Sage.

"What are you doing here?" Dan directed the question at Sage.

Gavin didn't like the man's tone. He was about to reply when Sage cut in.

"I brought papers for Gavin to sign." She held up the camera. "And to take pictures for our files."

Dan made a noncommittal grunt, then went over to the railing and peered through the bars.

Sage's mouth tightened with suppressed tension.

"Why don't you wait for me in the house," Gavin said in a low voice, his back to Dan. "The door's unlocked. There's leftover sandwiches in the fridge if you're hungry or help yourself to a cold drink."

"I will not run and hide," she said between clenched teeth.

He admired her tenacity. "That's my girl."

"Nice-looking horse," Dan commented when Gavin went to stand with him at the railing.

They discussed the horse's merits, along with the problems they would face breaking him to ride.

"I'll start tomorrow," Dan said.

Gavin's hackles rose. "We agreed that Ethan would be the one to train him."

"Your brother's got a bum leg."

Sage inhaled sharply.

"Which doesn't slow him down one bit," Gavin replied.

"This horse is too valuable to risk screwing him up."

Okay, now Gavin was mad. Dan typically talked tough, it was part of his two-faced salesman personality. Insults, however, were another matter.

"Ethan's the best there is with a horse in these parts."

"That's debatable." Challenge sparked in Dan's eyes.

He had Gavin over something of a barrel, and they both knew it. Without Dan's money, Gavin couldn't afford to construct the mare motel, which would cost in the tens of thousands of dollars.

For the second time in recent days, he felt trapped by his and Dan's partnership agreement.

"No reason you and Ethan can't work together."

Dan made another disgruntled sound. After a few more minutes of observing the mustang, he announced, "I have an appointment with a client," and left without so much as a "See you later."

The air surrounding Gavin and Sage felt suddenly lighter and clearer.

"Let's get out of here." He took her arm.

"Are you sure? It might not be a good idea to be seen with me. Someone's bound to tell Dan."

"At the moment, I don't care about him."

"Strong words for someone you're in partnership with."

"Yeah, well, that remains to be seen."

SAGE SET HER BRIEFCASE on the kitchen table and removed her jacket. After Dan's rude behavior at the round pen, she'd expected to be distraught, if not downright furious. She was neither. Something inside her had changed the past few days. Dan was losing his ability to yank her emotional chains.

It was a step. A huge one.

She glanced over at Gavin, a tenderness stirring inside her. He was responsible for this change in her. At least, in part.

"Water?" he asked, opening the fridge.

"Thanks."

He plucked two bottles from the shelf and handed one to her. It was then she noticed the scowl.

"Are you upset about Dan?" she asked.

"I don't like the way he treated you. Or his attitude." Shrugging off his jacket, he hung it on the coatrack. His hat landed on the countertop.

"Me, either. But it could have been much worse."

"I don't see how."

She unscrewed the lid on her water. "Attitude aside, he wasn't argumentative and he didn't make a scene. Which is more than I can say for the last two times he and I were together."

"I can't believe he insisted on breaking the mustang." Gavin braced his hands on the countertop. "That wasn't in our original agreement."

"It's because you're getting all the attention. And new customers. He doesn't like that." When Gavin didn't respond,

Sage went over and placed a hand atop his. "I'd say forget about him, but he's your partner and you can't. So do the next best thing. Forget about him *for now*."

"He shouldn't have talked to you the way he did," Gavin repeated.

"With any luck, it'll be the last time he talks to me for a while."

"What about Isa?"

Sage removed her hand. They really should be going over the adoption paperwork. She'd promised her cousin she'd be home by four.

"She hasn't mentioned Dan since our talk yesterday after the paternity test. I think once we get home, I'm going to have her see a counselor. A professional can probably help her deal with Dan's rejection better than I can."

"We, my family, saw a counselor before and after my mother's heart transplant surgery and again when she died. He did a lot for us. For me and Ethan and Sierra. Dad's still struggling."

Wanting to dispel the somber mood they'd fallen into, Sage opened her briefcase and removed a manila folder. Before she could lay the papers out on the table, Gavin removed the folder from her grasp and tossed it aside.

"We need to go over those," she protested.

He took her by the shoulders and held her in front of him, his intense gaze boring into her. "It's not just Dan. I wouldn't let anyone or anything hurt you, Sage. Not if I could help it."

"I know that." And she did. She trusted him. It should have come as a surprise considering they'd met only a short time ago. Somehow, it didn't.

"I can give you a dozen reasons why a relationship between us won't work." He paused, drew a breath.

"Are you asking me out?" she blurted.

"To start with." He raised his hand to her face and brushed away a stray tendril of hair. "We can go from there."

"Gavin, I..."

"Don't say no. Not without giving me a chance."

"I wasn't going to say no."

His mouth lifted in a half smile. "You weren't?"

"These last days at the ranch, capturing the mustang, being with you, your family, they've been the best I've had in over four years."

"Even with the arguing?"

"Even with that." She looked away, suddenly shy. "I'm not sure I can walk away."

"Don't."

Whatever else was on her mind to say would have to wait because he kissed her then and conversing was the last thing on her mind.

This wasn't their first kiss, yet, in light of their recent confessions, it felt like it. Discovering how much he cared, that he, too, wanted to continue seeing her, ignited a new intimacy between them. A connection that wasn't there before.

Within seconds, the kiss went from warm and tender to off-the-charts hot. When his lips abandoned hers to seek the sensitive skin beneath her ear and along the column of her neck, she let out a tiny, needy moan. Her body, responding without any direction from her, curled into him.

He kissed her again, groaned, then pulled away. She saw the lines of tension etched in his face, recognized the effort it took for him to exercise control.

"Gavin?"

"We should probably quit while we still can. While I still can."

He desired her *and* cared about her. The combination was a heady one and gave her the courage to voice what was in her heart.

"Why?" She slipped into his arms, aligned her hips with his. "You did say your family would be gone for hours."

That was all the persuading he needed. Scooping her up, he held her against his chest. She stifled a laugh. No man had picked her up like this since…maybe not ever.

He carried her out the kitchen, through a rustic great room and down the hall. She caught only glimpses of the house as they stole into its recesses. Photographs and pictures adorning the walls. A bathroom with—was that a claw-foot bathtub? Doors leading to bedrooms, one with clothes strewn over the floor and plastic horse figurines on a bookcase that had to be Cassie's.

At the last doorway he stopped and gazed down at her questioningly.

He was giving her the chance to say no. She could and there would be no repercussions. Gavin was above all an honorable and decent man.

"Put me down," she said. "Please."

He did as she requested, disappointment and acceptance in his eyes.

"Not here, silly!" Really, he was so sweet. Something of a dolt at times, but sweet. "On the bed."

He picked her up again. "You're going to drive me crazy."

How did he know that was her plan exactly?

The bedroom was large, more like a suite. A set of French doors, bracketed by a pair of sheer drapes, looked out onto the courtyard where she and Gavin had sat and talked the other day. In the center of the room was a queen-size four-poster bed, probably constructed by Gavin's father or grandfather. Shutting the door with his foot, he crossed the room and lowered her onto the patchwork quilt spread. The room was neither messy nor tidy but rather a comfortable in-between.

He stood over her, his hands at his sides, his gaze casting about.

"Wait here."

Wait? Sage pushed to a sitting position, instantly alarmed. Maybe *he* was having second thoughts.

Going to the armoire, he opened the door, pulled out a drawer and rummaged through the contents.

Ah! He wasn't having second thoughts at all.

Finding what he was searching for, he came back to the bed. "Sorry about that." He dropped a condom packet on the nightstand.

Sage looked over at it and burst into laughter as she read the name aloud. "Rainbow Delight?"

"It's a long story. Has to do with a high school buddy's bachelor party last spring."

"I can't wait to hear it."

He tugged at his shirt, yanking it from his pants. "It's the only condom I've got. If you don't—"

"Are you kidding?" She jumped to her feet and reached for the top button on his shirt, quickly unfastening it. "I happen to love rainbow colors."

No sooner did Gavin have his shirt off than he went to work on hers. Once she was out of it, he lowered her onto the quilt. In one easy motion, he removed her boots. Then her jeans.

"Nice," he murmured, his expression darkening as he took in the sight of her wearing just her bra and panties.

It wasn't fair that he should have all the fun.

"Come here, cowboy." Looping her arms around his neck, she tugged him down on top of her. His weight felt good as they sank together onto the mattress.

The remainder of their clothes disappeared in a blur.

"Cold?" he asked, covering her body with his. "We can get under the covers."

"No. This is perfect."

She snuggled deeper into his embrace, not wanting to miss the sight of Gavin fully naked for anything, even a little chill. He was splendid. Long, lean limbs. Hard muscled planes. Strength coupled with gentleness. Male perfection at its finest.

He seemed to appreciate her every bit as much as she did him. Skimming his hand along the length of her, he explored the hollow at the small of her back, the curve of her hip, the subtle expanse of her thigh.

"You're so beautiful."

She started to object, then decided not to. He was telling the truth. She could see it in his face. Hear it in his voice. To him, she was beautiful.

"Make love to me, Gavin," she murmured, lifting her hips in invitation as she brought his mouth to hers.

He groaned in response, his hands moving more frantically now. Kneading her breasts, cupping her buttocks, sliding between her legs. Then, his mouth was everywhere his hands had been, tasting, teasing, coaxing soft sounds from her.

She murmured his name, urged him to stop, then pleaded with him not to. His hands, his mouth, his warm breath caressing her soft feminine folds, became too much. She quickly climbed toward climax. A moment later, she tumbled over the edge—only to fall softly.

"That was…mmm."

He slowly kissed his way up the length of her body until they lay face-to-face, their legs entwined. "I agree."

Closing her fingers around his erection, she began stroking him. "You're beautiful, too."

He smiled.

It promptly vanished when she told him to, "Lie back," and took him into her mouth. He stopped her after only a few minutes.

"Party pooper," she complained.

"Darling, the party's just starting."

He pressed her into the mattress, simultaneously reaching for the condom on the nightstand. Sheathing himself, he parted her legs and entered her. The sensation of him filling her, stretching her, was exquisite. And addictive.

She wrapped her legs around his middle, arched her back. There was no slowing down. Neither of them tried. Moments later, she sensed his muscles tightening.

"Sage." He lifted his head, sought her gaze and held it fast.

Emotions exploded inside her. This was what it should be like between a man and a woman. What it had never been like for her before.

Gavin. He made the difference.

He clung to her and buried his face in her neck. She held him tight as he found his release. Soon, his breathing slowed, and he started to roll off her.

"No."

"I'm too heavy."

"I don't care."

"Sage."

She liked all the different ways he said her name. In anger. Frustration. Affection. Tenderly. She liked the way he said it in the throes of passion the best.

"What?" She sifted her fingers through his hair, sunlight from the window glinted off the black strands.

"We're going to figure things out. With us."

"I'm not worried."

"We have the mustang. Dan's going to pay you the back child support. Everything will work out."

Her response was to give him a peck on the lips.

Within seconds they were back where they started, hands frantically roaming and hungry for each other.

"Sure there aren't any more of those rainbow color condoms left?" she purred.

"I'll look."

He got up, only to go still.

"Is something the matter?"

"Listen."

A door slammed in another part of the house, followed by voices.

"Oh, shit." Sage started scrambling, digging through the quilt for her underwear. "Someone's home."

"It's just Cassie and my dad."

"*Just* Cassie and your dad?" Where the hell was her bra? "I will not be caught in bed with you."

Gavin laughed.

"This isn't funny."

"Relax." He bent and helped her gather their clothes. "I have an idea."

"It had better be a good one." She squirmed into her panties.

He nodded at the French doors.

It just might work, she thought.

Dressing as quietly as possible, they tiptoed out the French doors and into the courtyard. Sage winced when the latch made a loud noise as it clicked shut. Outside, she went weak. They were going to pull this off.

"Dammit!" She slapped her forehead.

"What?"

"My jacket and briefcase are in the kitchen. Your family's going to know."

"Relax."

"I can't."

Gavin grinned and hooked her by the arm. "Come on."

"How's my hair?"

"A lost cause."

Great. Just great.

They hurried around the house to the kitchen door, Sage attempting to finger comb her hair with one hand. The moment of truth came too soon. She prepared herself to be the object of curious stares and the subject of much speculation.

Except Cassie and Gavin's dad, who were busy unloading groceries, didn't seem the least bit surprised to see her or notice that anything was amiss.

She was almost let down. Almost.

Chapter Thirteen

Sage couldn't stop shaking. It was over. Finally. Not just the meeting, which had lasted an hour, but the whole wretched ordeal.

"Congratulations, *primita*." Roberto slung an arm over her shoulders as they walked from the upscale office building in north Scottsdale to the parking lot.

"Thank you so much." She smiled up at her cousin-in-law. "I really appreciate everything you've done for me and Isa."

The paternity test results had arrived bright and early that morning. Dan wasted no time. His attorney—Sage hadn't realized he retained one—contacted Roberto, and a meeting was set up for after lunch.

"I'm just glad it's over and done with," Roberto said. "Now you can enjoy the rest of your vacation. Speaking of which, what are you going to do?"

"I haven't thought about it." What a lie! Until the call from Dan's attorney, she'd been thinking of Gavin and their incredible afternoon together yesterday almost to exclusion.

He'd called her last night and again this morning. They'd talked like a couple of teenagers, soft and low. He'd chuckled, she'd giggled. Isa had looked at Sage in confusion while her cousin Anna rolled her eyes knowingly.

Sage couldn't remember the last time she'd felt so young. Or, so good. What should have been an embarrassing situation when they were nearly caught by Gavin's dad and daughter had turned into an enjoyable dinner with the family, followed by several goodbye kisses that left Sage walking on air—or should she say, driving on air—the entire ride home to her cousin's.

She decided to enjoy it while it lasted. Once she returned to Show Low and two hundred miles separated her and Gavin, it would be difficult to recapture the feelings she was having now.

"I've got another appointment." Roberto kissed her on the cheek, said, "See you tonight" and then headed to his car.

Sage waved at him before getting into her truck. She'd barely started the engine when her cell phone rang.

"Hi." She cradled the phone to her ear, anticipating hearing the rich timbre of Gavin's voice.

"Did I interrupt you?"

"We just finished the meeting."

"How'd it go?"

"Unbelievably well. Dan and I agreed on a new monthly amount, and he's going to pay an additional sum toward the back child support he owes. It'll take him almost three years to catch up, but at least Isa will have the money."

"That's great. I'm really happy for you both."

Unfortunately, there was always a downside. "I just wish Dan wanted to see her."

"He still doesn't?"

"No. I agreed to visitation, naturally, and we came up with a schedule. He made it clear Isa wasn't to come here. If anything, he'd go to Show Low. I got the impression that wasn't going to happen very often."

"Poor kid."

"Has he said anything to you?" Sage inserted her key in the ignition.

"About Isa?"

"No. The mustang or your partnership." She hadn't mentioned Dan's remark about his money being tied up elsewhere.

"We talked this morning. Decided on which mares we'd breed first and set a price for stud fees. He has a few clients interested."

"Okay, good." She relaxed. It was impossible for her not to dwell on what effect her relationship with Gavin would have on his and Dan's. Not that Dan knew anything—or ever would if she could help it.

"I finished filling out the adoption paperwork. Was thinking maybe I could drop it off tonight."

"You don't have to drive all the way into Scottsdale for that."

"I wasn't. I was going to drive all the way into Scottsdale to pick you up for dinner."

"Really?" She brightened.

"Ever been to P.F. Chang's?"

"Once. I love Chinese food." Sage mentally rummaged through her suitcase contents and the clothes she'd brought with her. No dresses or shoes besides boots and sneakers. Maybe Anna had a dress and a pair of heels she could borrow that were suitable for fine dining.

"Six o'clock okay?"

She held the phone closer, imagining Gavin in dress clothes. He would leave her breathless. "Perfect. See you then."

Grinning foolishly, she started the truck and headed toward the exit. She hadn't quite reached it when her phone rang again. Ready to ask Gavin what he'd forgotten, she slowed when she recognized her boss's number.

"Hi, Steve. Did you get the pictures I emailed?"

"Yeah, thanks. They're great."

"I just got off the phone with Gavin Powell." Since Steve's conversations usually lasted several minutes, she pulled into the nearest empty parking space. "He's completed the adoption papers. I'll get them later today and overnight them tomorrow."

"Forget it. You don't need to bother with that. There's been a change in plans."

Sage didn't like the tone in Steve's voice. She'd heard it before, and it usually preceded the delivery of bad news. "What change?"

"We're going to follow regular procedure with the mustang. Auction him to the public."

"W-why?"

"The media attention. Did you watch TV last night?"

"A little."

She'd seen the evening broadcast at Gavin's. Both broadcasts, in fact. Everyone had crowded together in the great room, laughing and ribbing Gavin mercilessly. They'd also congratulated him on doing such a great job.

"This horse has made big news, and not just statewide," Steve continued. "National, too. One clip's gone viral on the internet. The office can't keep up with all the phone calls."

"What does that have to do with Gavin Powell adopting him?"

"Money, of course. With all the media attention, this horse will bring a considerably higher price than usual at auction. And positive publicity for the bureau. We can use both."

"But you already agreed," she protested, anticipating Gavin's reaction.

He would be devastated. And angry. At the BLM and also at her. Hadn't she assured him there would be no problem adopting the mustang?

"Nothing's in writing," Steve said, easily dismissing her objection.

"You gave your word."

"Even if I wanted to let Powell adopt the horse, which I

don't, it's out of my hands. The head of the department won't let an opportunity like this one slip by without making the most of it."

Sage rubbed her aching forehead. All she could think of was Gavin. His plans, his dreams, his hopes for the future about to disintegrate before his eyes.

"You can't do this, Steve. Please. Gavin Powell and his family are the ones who captured the mustang, and it wasn't easy. More than that, he's the one who originally contacted the BLM. We owe him."

"He still can own the horse. He just has to win him at the auction."

Except Sage knew the Powells didn't have the money. Not if the mustang went for the large sum Steve and the department head were obviously hoping he'd bring.

"It's not fair."

"Few things in life are," Steve answered caustically. "Why do you care anyway?"

"The Powells are nice people." She hoped he didn't notice the hitch in her voice. "And we—I—promised them."

She considered going above Steve's head, making a case on the Powells' behalf to the head of the department. Except what good would that do? As Steve had said, it was the head of the department who'd decided to publically auction the mustang.

Damn, damn, damn! This couldn't be happening.

She closed her eyes, holding her tears at bay, guilt tearing her up inside.

"Do you have Powell's number?" Steve asked. "I'm going to call him now."

"No! Let me tell him."

The news would be bad enough. Worse coming from a stranger. Besides, this was her fault and her responsibility to handle. Afterward, she'd advise Gavin on the ins and outs of the auction, help him prepare.

At least he'd have the coming week. In that time, Gavin could breed the mustang to a few of his mares.

Then, she remembered. Avaro was in heat. She'd probably mated with the mustang during their little adventure. They could breed Avaro to the mustang again, just to make sure. And Sage would give Gavin the foal. There was also the new business he was getting because of finding the mustang. It wasn't all bad, she reasoned.

Only she doubted Gavin would see it that way. Nothing could make up for losing the mustang.

"Are you sure?" Steve asked. "I'd be happy to call him."

Sage glanced at her watch, made a mental note to call her cousin and check on Isa. "I'm on my way there now."

"Okay. I'll see you tomorrow."

"Tomorrow?" Her heart jumped. "Are you coming to Mustang Valley?"

"No, you're bringing the horse here."

"I…I'm on vacation."

"Not till Friday. Which means you're on the BLM's clock through tomorrow. We need you to transport the horse here as soon as possible so we can begin processing him. PR wants to really pump up the advertising. The auction's a week from Saturday. We don't have much time."

"Steve." Sage was aware of the pleading in her voice. "Give the Powells a few days with the horse. I'll bring him up Monday morning."

"Impossible."

She had no choice. Not if she wanted to keep her job. The idea of rebelling, of telling her boss to shove it, was appealing. Also unrealistic. She had a daughter to support and eight years with the BLM. Decent jobs like hers, ones with benefits, weren't easy to come by.

"Fine," she said, sick to the bottom of her soul. "I'll call you tomorrow when I'm on the road."

Wiping her watery eyes, she put the truck in gear and drove to Powell Ranch. After calling Anna and telling her she'd be late, Sage concentrated on coming up with the best and kindest way to tell Gavin about the mustang. In the end, she decided to be honest and straightforward. Sugarcoating or dancing around the topic wouldn't lessen the terrible blow, merely postpone it.

Gavin was nowhere to be seen when she arrived at the ranch and parked. Spying Javier leaving the arena on horseback, she went after him. A glance at the empty round pen made her think the mustang had been moved to a more permanent location.

Except it wouldn't be permanent.

Javier told her Gavin had gotten a phone call a little bit ago and went into the house. She resisted the urge to run, choosing a brisk walk instead. At the back door, she knocked. And knocked again. In between she chewed a thumbnail. Where was he?

At last, Gavin answered the door. His cell phone dangling from his fingers.

"Hey, what are you doing here?"

"I dropped by to—" The stunned look he wore stopped her. She stepped over the threshold, afraid Steve had changed his mind and called Gavin about the mustang. "Is everything all right?"

"No." He motioned her inside. "I just got off the phone with—"

"I'm sorry," she blurted, and threw herself in his arms.

"You know?"

"Yes, my boss called me. I told him I wanted to tell you myself."

Gavin set her gently aside and held her at arm's length. "Tell me what?"

"About the mustang."

"I don't know what you're talking about."

"That wasn't my boss on the phone with you?"

He frowned in confusion. "Why would your boss call me?"

Oh, no! She'd jumped to the wrong conclusion. This wasn't going anything like she'd planned.

"Then who was it you were talking to?"

"Dan," Gavin said solemnly. "He's terminating our partnership agreement. Said he doesn't have the money now that he has to pay you the back child support."

The strength went out of Sage's legs. She stumbled to the table, pulled out a chair and dropped into it.

"That bastard," she said, covering her face with her hands. "That dirty bastard."

"I don't care. Not that much. He's been a pain in the ass from the beginning. And now I'm not so sure I need him anymore. Not with the mustang."

Sage groaned.

Gavin sat in the chair next to hers. "What's wrong, honey?"

He was being so nice. She didn't deserve it. "This is terrible. Awful. I'm still in shock."

"Forget it. Dan's not worth the trouble."

"Not Dan." She reached for Gavin's hand and folded it between hers. "My boss called me right after I talked to you. He's ordered me to transport the mustang to our Show Low facility. Tomorrow."

He sat back. "Why?"

"Because he's...the mustang...is going to be publically auctioned a week from Saturday. The department head changed his mind. They aren't going to let you adopt the mustang outright."

He stared at her, disbelief written on his face.

"You'll have to bid on him like everyone else. I'm sorry." She squeezed his fingers. "I would give anything for this not to have happened."

Gavin stood, went over to the sink and looked out the window.

Sage sat, waiting quietly, respecting his need for a few minutes to himself.

When he turned to her, his expression was that of a defeated man.

She rushed to him and hugged him fiercely.

While he held her in return, the strength and passion and conviction that was Gavin had seeped out of him.

THE MUSTANG DIDN'T WANT TO GO in Sage's trailer. That made two of them. Gavin didn't want the mustang to go in Sage's trailer, either.

As she'd informed him yesterday, Gavin had no choice. According to the law, the mustang belonged to the federal government. If he tried to harbor the horse illegally, there would be serious repercussions. So, he complied, as much as it galled him.

"Watch out!" Ethan called a split second before the mustang's right rear hoof sliced the air in what was two inches shy of a deadly kick.

It had taken five of them, Gavin, Ethan, their dad, Sage and Javier, forty minutes to put a halter on the horse and drag him to the trailer. Gavin's shoulders would be sore for a week, and his dad sported a bright red welt across his wrist. If not for the gloves they all wore, their palms would be ripped to shreds from rope burns.

"Let's try this again."

Gavin positioned himself to the right of the mustang and tossed his rope to Javier on the other side. Ethan gripped the rope attached to the mustang's halter and wound it around an opening in the side of Sage's trailer. The two of them proceeded to engage each other in a game of tug-of-war, with the mustang having the advantage.

Slowly, Gavin and Javier drew their rope taut across the mustang's hindquarters. They were ready for him when he bucked. They were also ready for him when he stopped.

"Now!"

Knowing he'd want to escape the rope irritating his back legs, they forced him forward one reluctant step at a time. Ethan aided the process by pulling on the lead rope. The mustang resisted, grunting and squealing and putting all his weight in his back legs until he was almost sitting on the ground. Exhaustion eventually wore him down.

No graceful entrance into the trailer for him. He charged ahead, landing with a resounding thud and banging into the sidewall.

Sage, who had been waiting for just this moment, slammed the trailer door shut behind him.

They breathed a collective sigh of relief. So did the crowd that had gathered to watch.

"Good job, Dad." Cassie ran over to peer at the mustang through the open slats in the trailer.

"Not so close," Gavin warned her, taking off his gloves and wiping his damp forehead with his sleeve. To Sage, he said, "I'll be glad when school starts up again next week."

"No, you won't. You like having her around."

She was right. "Maybe I should go with you. He could give you trouble on the drive."

"I'd like that except…" She smiled sadly.

"More BLM policy?"

"'Fraid so. I can't even take Isa with me."

"Call me when you get there."

"I will." She made her farewells to Gavin's family, promising to see them tomorrow.

He slung an arm over her shoulders and walked her to the cab of her truck. No one paid them much attention, evidently accepting that he and Sage were a couple and deserved a private goodbye.

"I'm sorry."

"For what?" he asked.

"This." She waved a hand at the trailer and mustang. "It's all my fault."

"I don't see how."

"I promised you ownership."

"None of us saw this coming."

"You have every right to be mad at me."

"I'm not."

No, he wasn't mad at her. But Dan? Hell, yes. For his treatment of her and Isa, and the slimy way he'd terminated their partnership agreement.

Gavin was also mad at himself. Like his father, he'd put his trust in someone untrustworthy, blinded by the prospect of easy money.

"It's ironic," Sage said. "If the girls didn't wander off, we might not have captured the mustang for weeks. It was them being found in the canyon with him that's generated all the media attention. Otherwise, he'd be just another feral horse."

"Yeah." Ironic and unlucky.

"What are you going to do?"

"I'm not sure." A lot had happened in the past day, and he'd yet to process it all.

She circled his waist with her arms and rested her head on his chest.

He stroked her hair, which she wore loose rather than in her customary ponytail. He enjoyed running his fingers through its thickness, pictured it fanned out on his pillow.

"I'll miss you."

"Me, too," she murmured, her face pressed into his jacket.

One thing they had agreed on last night was that Sage would return to Mustang Valley after dropping off the horse. Not only to finish her vacation but to be with him. Where they'd go with their relationship from there remained to be seen.

"Not to pressure you, but I really hope you'll go to the auction. If only so we can spend the weekend together."

"Now, there's an offer I can't refuse."

The truth was, he had a lot to consider before deciding. On the one hand, it would kill him to watch someone else buy the mustang. On the other hand, it would kill him worse if the going price turned out to be something he could have afforded and he wasn't there.

If only he was more certain the potential new customers who'd called or come by would still be interested in doing business even if the mustang wasn't on the ranch. If only he had a spare couple thousand dollars tucked away somewhere.

"I hate to go." Sage expelled a long, mournful breath. "But I need to leave now if I don't want to be driving that highway at midnight."

Hooking a finger under her chin, he lifted her face to his. Their relationship was still brand-new and each kiss an exciting discovery.

Would it still be like this when they'd kissed a hundred times? A thousand?

If he wanted a future with Sage, and he did, he needed something worthwhile to offer her. Financial stability. A decent home in good repair. A profitable livelihood. Owning and operating a successful stud and breeding business could provide all that and more.

As long as he had a worthy stallion.

Preferably the mustang.

After yet another kiss, a "Drive careful" and last smile, he stood and watched as Sage drove away, the horse trailer bumping along behind her truck.

Seeing his brother strolling toward the stables, Gavin hollered to him. "Ethan!"

"What's up?" he asked when Gavin drew near, buckling the front of his farrier chaps.

"I'm calling a family meeting."

"Now?"

"Yeah, now." They hadn't had one since after their mother died.

"About what?"

"The mustang. I want to buy him at the auction."

Ethan grinned. "Let's do it!"

Their dad made a pot of fresh coffee for the meeting, which took place an hour later at the kitchen table. It was just like the ones they had years before, except instead of Sierra sitting to Gavin's left, his daughter did.

She'd been surprised when he asked her to take part in the meeting. "You're family," he'd said in response, and she smiled even bigger than when he'd given her Blue.

Maybe he'd get the hang of this parenting thing, after all.

Gavin laid out the files containing the ranch's bank statements and past year's income and expense reports in the middle of the table.

"Does Sage have any idea how much the mustang will go for?" his father asked after Gavin had summarized the condition of their current finances.

"Not really. She says the BLM has never had a situation like this before."

"I don't think the horse will go for that much," Ethan said confidently. "Sure, he's a novelty and generated a lot of attention. But once people see what a handful he is, they'll rethink owning him."

Gavin hoped his brother was right. "What we have to figure out is how much cash we can raise without putting the ranch or the family in jeopardy."

They debated the issue hotly for some time, rereviewing the income and expense reports, making projections for the next year and brainstorming ideas on how to increase revenues and cut corners.

Finally, they decided on an amount. Gavin wasn't sure it would be enough.

"I have some money set aside," his father said quietly. "I want you to have it."

"You sure, Dad?"

"It's not much. Twelve hundred dollars. Leftover from your mother's life insurance policy. I know she'd want you to have it."

Gavin was deeply touched. "Thank you."

"I have some money, too," Cassie piped up. "Fifty-three dollars and twenty-five cents. From babysitting."

"Sweetheart, I don't want to take your money."

"You said I was family."

"Yes, but—"

"I want to help, too. I can get more babysitting jobs." She gazed at him with heartfelt earnestness.

Gavin tried to figure out what he'd done to deserve such a fantastic kid.

"Okay. Thank you." Because it meant so much to her, he'd accept her babysitting money and make it up to her another way.

"I guess that's it." Ethan lifted his coffee mug in a toast.

Cathy McDavid 185

Everyone clinked mugs, except Cassie. She raised her glass of juice.

Gavin glanced around the table, astounded at the differences one short week had made in their lives.

The mustang had managed to unite them as a family, give them a shared dream, help Gavin and Cassie grow closer and, maybe most important, bring Sage to him.

This was only the beginning. There were more changes, good ones, on the way. He could feel it.

All he had to do was outbid the competition at the auction.

Chapter Fourteen

Gavin fingered the piece of card stock in his hand. On it was printed his number—one hundred and twenty-nine. So many bidders. He'd seen one individual with a number well into the two hundreds. And at least three times as many spectators were in attendance. According to talk, this was the most well-attended auction in the history of the BLM.

It was also the first one with TV news reporters and camera operators.

"Where's Sage?" Cassie asked, holding on to Gavin's hand as they strolled the auction grounds.

Ethan and their dad stayed behind to run the ranch. While Gavin was pleased his dad was taking a more active role in the family business, he missed the home-cooked meals. Frozen pizza and microwave lasagna just didn't taste as good.

"I don't know." Gavin scanned the crowd for Sage. He considered calling her cell phone then decided against it. She was working today. "She said she'd find us before the auction started."

Which was half an hour away.

The knot in Gavin's stomach tightened. All the assurances Sage had given him this past week weren't enough to relieve his agitation.

"Cassie!"

At the sound of her name being called, both Cassie and

Gavin came to a halt. Isa appeared, running toward them and dragging her aunt Anna and uncle Roberto with her. Gavin had met Sage's cousin and cousin-in-law twice during the past week and liked them very much. He thought they might like him, too.

"Hi," Anna said a little breathlessly when they met up.

"Good to see you again." Gavin shook Roberto's hand. "I didn't know you were coming."

"Spur-of-the-moment decision."

"Dad and I drove up last night," Cassie announced over the top of Isa's head. The younger girl had attached herself to Cassie, and they'd need a crowbar to pry them apart.

"Have you seen the mustang yet?" Anna asked.

"Several times."

Gavin had planted himself at the mustang's pen shortly after the main gate was opened and stayed put for nearly an hour. As much as he'd wanted to, he couldn't prevent other people from inspecting the horse—from outside the pen. No one dared step inside, not if they valued their safety. Gavin secretly cheered the mustang's aggressive temperament. Anything to make him less appealing to prospective bidders.

"We thought we'd walk over to see him." Roberto craned his neck in the direction of the horse pens.

"Cassie and I will go with you," Gavin offered.

He commented on several of the other horses up for auction as they walked down the long aisle between the pens. Anna and Roberto murmured polite replies, typical of nonhorse enthusiasts.

"Isa, check out these horses." Cassie and Isa darted to a pen containing two mares, one gray, one paint. "My dad's buying them."

"Are you?" Roberto asked.

"Maybe." Gavin came up behind Cassie. "If they sell for

the right price. I'm trying to preserve mustang bloodlines, and I'm thinking they might make good breeding stock."

All the broodmares in the world wouldn't do him any good if he didn't win the mustang.

He'd transferred four thousand dollars into the ranch's checking account yesterday. Surely that would be enough. Sage seemed to think it was four or five times the amount he'd need.

The mustang had been placed in a separate pen, far away from the other horses. Spectators were standing two and three deep when they got there, an increase from earlier.

Anna, Roberto and the girls wormed their way closer. Gavin stayed behind, glimpsing the mustang now and again when someone moved. Lights flashed as cameras went off. Annoyed at the unwanted attention, the mustang lowered his head and pawed the ground.

A young man with more brawn than brains reached through the bars and barely escaped having his hand bitten.

Soon, Gavin thought, this will all be over and I'll take my horse home.

"I'm hungry," Isa complained some minutes later when the thrill had worn off for her.

"Me, too." Roberto pressed a finger to the tip of her nose.

"If we're going to eat," Gavin said, "maybe we should do it before the auction starts." He wasn't really hungry but he could use a cold drink.

After finishing their meal of hot dogs and potato chips, they made their way to the bleachers, which were already two-thirds filled, and found seats that afforded them a decent view.

Gavin's phone rang soon after they were seated. "It's Sage," he said, and answered, "Hey."

"Where are you?"

"In the stands." He told her which section. "Can you get away?"

"No. Not till later, unfortunately."

He could hear the disappointment in her voice. It matched his own.

What would it be like when he returned to the valley tomorrow and she remained in Show Low?

They'd talk tonight. Make some definite plans. No, tomorrow would be soon enough. He'd rather celebrate tonight, which they would. In style.

"Call me when you're done. We'll meet you by the chuck wagon."

"Good luck," she said, her voice soft and warm. "But I know you won't need it. That horse is yours, Gavin. He's been yours from the moment you saw him."

He felt the same way.

Pocketing his phone, Gavin reread the auction flyer for the third time, only to be distracted by a lone man climbing the bleacher stairs. He didn't look like the usual horse auction patron, not with his tailored slacks, dress shoes and expensive jacket.

As he took a seat three rows in front of them, he turned to speak to an old-timer beside him.

"James," Roberto suddenly called out. "James Bridwell."

Glancing behind him, the man gave a brief wave of acknowledgment when he spied Roberto.

"You know him?" Anna asked.

Gavin was wondering the same thing.

"We run into each other on occasion. He's an attorney with a firm in Scottsdale."

An uneasiness Gavin couldn't explain came over him. Why should it matter that an attorney from Scottsdale was at a BLM horse auction?

Except he couldn't shake the feeling that it *did* matter. A lot.

The feeling intensified when he noticed the man also held a card stock bidder's number.

"SOLD TO BIDDER…"

Gavin held up his number for the auctioneer to see.

"129."

"You won!" Cassie tugged on his jacket sleeve.

He smiled down at her, admittedly caught up in the excitement. "We probably don't need another mare."

Except he would need them, when he brought the mustang home.

As Sage had predicted, the horses at the auction were all going for one to two hundred dollars despite the enormous crowd. Gavin dared to hope. Surely the mustang wouldn't bring much more than that. He patted his pocket, the one containing his checkbook, and thought again of the balance.

It would be enough.

The attorney sitting in front of them hadn't bid on one single horse. He wasn't alone. According to the snippets of conversation Gavin picked up from his neighbors, many people had come solely to see the mustang auctioned.

He tried to shake off his uneasiness, telling himself the attorney wasn't important.

The auction continued. Thirty minute went by. Forty-five. At one point, the auctioneer's singsong voice started to crack. Burros, managing to be both scruffy and adorable at the same time, were also sold. Cassie was naturally enamored, as was most of the crowd, and wanted one.

Finally, they announced the mustang was up next for bid. Excitement rippled through the stands, and the noise level instantly increased. Gavin's right leg beat a frenzied tattoo.

A minute passed. Then three. Clanging noises came from

the holding pens behind the auctioneer's booth, followed by shouting. More noise, more shouting, and the gate was at last thrown open.

The mustang emerged, and he was none too happy.

Nostrils flaring, feet prancing, head shaking, he fought the three men who dared try to restrain him with their ropes. Oohs, aahs and whistles emanated from the crowd, which incited the mustang even more. The wranglers, three of them, did their best to control a living, breathing tornado.

Sage entered the arena behind the men and horse, acting as an extra hand and spotter in case of trouble.

Gavin paid little attention while the auctioneer extolled the mustang's merits. Everything and everyone took on a strange, surreal quality. That changed the instant the bidding began.

The auctioneer called for five hundred dollars to start. When no one responded, he called for four hundred. Then three.

Someone offered two hundred. Like a gun shot at the start of a race, they were off. From that moment on, the bidding came fast and furious.

Gavin didn't jump right in. Instinct told him to wait and see what everyone else did first. Within seconds, the price jumped to six hundred. Then seven. He raised his number in the air. One of the auctioneer's helpers standing outside the arena saw him, pointed at him and called out his bid.

Immediately, he was beaten. He bid once more, only to be outbid again. Each time he went higher, vaguely aware that the price for the mustang had reached a thousand. Then two thousand. That was okay. He still had plenty of money.

One by one, the less serious bidders dropped out. When the going price reached three thousand dollars, only three people remained. Gavin, a middle-aged woman and the attorney.

The attorney?

Gavin had been too involved to realize the attorney had been bidding against him.

At thirty-five hundred dollars, the woman dropped out.

The mustang began to paw the ground impatiently as if urging Gavin to hurry up.

"Thirty-eight hundred," he called out.

"Do I have thirty-nine?" the auctioneer asked.

No one responded. The attorney was on his cell phone, speaking to someone.

Elation surged inside Gavin. His hands shook. The mustang was his!

In the arena, Sage grinned and gave him a thumbs-up sign.

"Going once, going twice—"

"Four thousand dollars," the attorney shouted.

"Do I hear forty-one hundred?"

Four thousand was all Gavin had in his checking account. Fighting panic, he called out, "Forty-five hundred." He couldn't lose the mustang. Not when he was this close. Somehow he'd come up with the other five hundred dollars.

Then, he remembered he'd also bought the two mares. Son of a bitch. He was screwed.

The attorney continued talking on his cell phone, then waved his hand wildly in the air.

"Five thousand dollars!"

"Going once," the auctioneer sang into the microphone.

There was no way Gavin could match that amount, much less beat it.

"Going twice."

Pain sliced through him. This couldn't be happening. The horse was supposed to go for hundreds of dollars, not thousands.

"Going three times."

He crumpled his card-stock number into a ball and threw it on the bleacher floor beneath his feet.

"Sold! To number 238."

The words rang like a death toll in Gavin's ears.

"GAVIN!"

He slowed at the sound of Sage's voice. Not that he'd been walking fast. He couldn't, his feet weighed a thousand pounds each.

She ran to where he, Anna, Roberto and the girls milled on the fringes of the thinning crowd.

"I couldn't get away any sooner," she explained in a rush. "I had to help the wranglers with…" She took his hand, pressed her free one to his cheek. "It's crazy. I still can't believe he went for that much money."

Gavin wanted to comfort her. She seemed to need it. Except there was only cold emptiness inside him.

"Do you know who bought him?" he asked in a flat voice.

"Not the owner's name. The man who bid on him was acting as an agent. I might be able to find out in a few days, once the paperwork is processed. Steve will tell me."

Her boss. The name penetrated the thick haze surrounding Gavin's brain.

"Cassie?" Where had she gone? He searched the immediate area, spotting the two girls with their heads together by the chuck wagon. "Come on, honey," he hollered. "We need to get on the road."

"You're leaving?" Sage asked. "So soon? I thought we'd… have some time together."

He'd thought that, too, when they were going to be celebrating.

"I need to get the mares home."

"That's right. You bought two new horses."

Breeding stock he wouldn't need now.

Dammit. The mustang was his. He'd tracked him, captured him, pinned his entire future on owning him.

"Can I help you load them?" Sage offered.

"I can manage, thanks."

On some level he recognized he was putting distance between him and Sage. She realized it, too.

"Please, Gavin. Talk to me before you go." Her fingers entwined in his were warm and coaxing.

Anna must have read the situation. "There's a little petting zoo right up the road. Why don't Roberto and I take the girls there?"

Sage smiled her thanks.

Gavin muttered a distracted "Okay." He was still reeling and really didn't want to talk to Sage. Or anyone for that matter.

She accompanied him to his truck and trailer. Climbing in, he drove very slowly through the grounds to the horse pens.

Loading the mares didn't take much time. Gavin had chosen well. For wild horses, these two possessed relatively calm dispositions as well as striking looks. It was a shame they wouldn't be able to combine their desirable qualities with those of the mustang.

All at once, the barrier holding his emotions in check broke. They crashed over him with a force that left him shaking. Anger. Frustration. Resentment. Disappointment.

Devastation.

He slammed the trailer door shut harder than necessary. The startled mares flinched and bunched toward the front.

"There are other feral stallions for sale," Sage said gently. "They come in all the time."

Gavin shook his head.

"I know they won't be the same—"

He cut her off. "I'm not interested in another horse."

"You may feel differently later."

"I'm not interested," he repeated harshly.

They got back in his truck and drove to the main parking lot. Anna and Roberto hadn't yet returned with the girls. Gavin selected a spot in the half-empty lot, parked and turned off the engine. He and Sage said nothing for several moments. He hoped it would last, that she would give him a break before pressuring him.

She didn't.

"I was thinking, I can relocate to Mustang Valley. Live with you, if you're willing," she added shyly. "My house is on a month-to-month lease so I can leave anytime. And I have family in the Phoenix area."

If the mustang were in the trailer with the mares, Gavin would be having an entirely different reaction. He'd grab Sage, kiss her, tell her how happy she made him. As it was, the cold emptiness inside him grew only colder.

"What about your job?"

"If the BLM doesn't have an opening in their Phoenix office, I'll find a new one."

She was going to make him say it, strip him of his pride and leave him bare to the bone.

"I can't afford to support you while you're looking."

"I wouldn't expect you to," she answered breezily. "I'll have extra money coming in now that Dan's paying me."

Gavin ground his teeth. He wished she hadn't brought up her ex's name. If he and Dan were still partners, Gavin would have been able to outbid the attorney.

"I'd rather you didn't live off his money."

"It's not like that. He owes me. I've supported Isa for years when he should have been paying."

Splitting hairs, in his opinion.

"Don't you want to keep seeing me?" She was finally getting past all his excuses and to the heart of the matter.

"*Keep* seeing you," he said. "Not be the reason you're up-rooting your entire life."

"I was thinking of it as more like creating a new one."

It was then he noticed the tears forming in her eyes.

Much as he wanted to, he wasn't ready to make the kind of commitment she was asking of him. He might have been, if the day had ended differently.

Instead, he said, "Let's talk about this in a week or two. After I've had a chance to meet with the family. Examine our options."

"You can still go ahead with the stud and breeding business." She looked at him appealingly. "With a new partner."

"Who?"

"Me."

He recoiled as if she'd slapped him across the face. "I won't take money from you."

"But you would from Dan."

"That was different."

"Why? Because he's a man?"

"Because he's not someone—" Gavin started to say, *I love,* but stopped himself. This wasn't the time to admit his feelings for Sage, give her cause to have expectations he couldn't meet. "Someone I have an intimate relationship with," he said instead.

He'd let her down. She'd been hoping for a declaration of love. Everything in her expression told him so.

Gavin shifted and stared out the driver's side window.

"You blame me for losing the mustang."

"No."

"I misled you. Assured you he'd sell for a fraction of what he did."

"Sage, I don't blame you."

Only he did. A little. He'd counted on her being right. On her experience and connections with the BLM. It wasn't anything he couldn't get over eventually. Her intentions had been honest and sincere, after all.

He probably wasn't being fair to her, but he'd lost so much today and wasn't thinking his clearest.

"I get that you don't want to take my money. I also get that you're a traditional kind of guy. That you feel a responsibility to take care of any woman in your life, even if she doesn't need taking care of."

He closed his eyes, wishing she would stop talking. Let him go home and sort through this mess before wringing a decision from him.

"We'd make really good partners," she went on, "if you think about it. I know we don't always agree, but look at it this way. Your strengths balance my weakness and vice versa."

"Sage—"

"I'll come down next Friday. We can hash out the details."

The more she pushed him, the more she made him feel like a complete failure.

"I don't want to think about this now," he snapped, hating himself for his lousy temper.

She pursed her lips, her way of asking when *did* he want to think about it?

"I would feel a whole lot better if we just didn't make any decisions for a while." He was surprised how reasonable his voice sounded considering the turmoil raging inside him.

At that moment, an SUV pulled up beside them. Not her cousin's vehicle. This one had a BLM insignia on the door.

"Oh, great," Sage muttered when a man stepped out and came over. "It's my boss." She opened the door and got out.

Gavin did, too, and she introduced them.

"Sage, I'm glad I found you before you left." He motioned for her to join him a few feet away. "You got a minute?"

Gavin shoved his hands in his jacket pockets and kicked

at a small rock at his feet. He didn't intend to eavesdrop, but Steve's deep voice carried.

"I need you to transport the mustang to the new owner tomorrow."

"Where?"

"Outside of Scottsdale. Not far from that place where you went on your vacation. I'll have the exact address for you in the morning."

Mustang Valley?

Learning that the new owner of the mustang lived near him and that Sage would be the one to deliver the horse was the final blow.

Gavin returned to his truck, vaguely aware that he was staggering.

What a fool he'd been, to think he could turn things around and create something significant for him and his family. His mother's illness had sent them into a downward spiral from which they would never recover. He should have known better than to try.

Without realizing how he'd got there, he found himself sitting behind the steering wheel, his hand on the key, poised to start the ignition. Wait. He couldn't leave. Cassie wasn't back yet.

He jerked when the passenger side door opened and Sage stood framed in it. "Steve's gone."

Sound came from his mouth, an unintelligible reply to her statement.

"Gavin, I…I'll refuse the assignment if you want me to. I just figured, well, I'll take good care of the horse."

He didn't answer. The fragmented thoughts whirling inside his head refused to come together into something coherent.

"I'll come by the ranch with I'm done."

Another SUV pulled into the parking lot then, this one her

cousin's. He saw Cassie in the backseat. She was reading a book to Isa.

Cassie.

She was his priority now.

Maybe he *should* consider buying a different wild stallion. Salvage as much of his original plan as he could.

"Gavin?" Sage leaned into the truck. "Did you hear me? I'll come by the ranch tomorrow."

He shook his head. At her confused expression, he got out and circled the truck.

She smiled when he reached for her. It disappeared when he held her at arm's length.

"You don't have to," he told her, striving to keep his voice gentle. He remembered that from when his mother was sick. The doctors had always delivered bad news in low, quiet tones. "In fact, it might be best if you didn't."

"What are you saying?"

"I care about you. More than you realize." He squeezed her shoulders. That was another thing the doctors had done. They'd placed reassuring hands on him and his family. "But we were foolish to ever think we could make a go of this."

Dismay filled her eyes. "We *can*."

"There are too many obstacles. The distance—"

"I told you, I'll move."

He shook his head. "I need time, Sage. I'm not the kind of person who can pluck a plan B out of the air. It's important that I build the business, the ranch and my home into something meaningful before I can share them with you."

"That's what people who care about each other do. They build meaningful homes and businesses. Together."

"I wasn't ready to be a father when Cassie was born. I loved her but I was incapable of giving her what she needed. I regret that and am doing my damnedest to make up for it."

"I know how important she is to you. I have a daughter, too."

"When I commit to you, Sage, it will be when we're both ready. Not before and not just you."

She stiffened. "How long will that take? Because some people are never ready and use it as a convenient excuse."

"I don't know." He wouldn't lie to her. "And asking you to wait is unfair."

"I would, you know." Her features crumbled.

He was probably committing a huge mistake by letting her go.

Hadn't he accused Dan of the same thing?

Pride was Gavin's downfall. A downfall of all the Powell men. He couldn't change the way he felt, however. Not even if it resulted in an end to his relationship with Sage.

The SUV door opened, and Cassie emerged.

"Dad?"

"Yeah, honey."

She walked toward him, casting uncertain glances at him and Sage. "Are we leaving?"

"In a minute."

"Bye, Ms. Navarre." She gave Sage a tentative wave, then continued to Gavin's truck. It was obvious from Cassie's woeful expression that she'd deduced at least some of what was happening. So, probably, had Anna and Roberto, for they didn't emerge from the SUV.

Sage tried to smile at Cassie. She couldn't, not with her lower lip trembling. "This isn't at all how I thought today would end," she said to Gavin, and wiped her nose.

"Me, either."

"I love you, Gavin, and I think you're making a terrible mistake."

His chest ached. He wished she hadn't said that. Wished he could say it back to her because it was true.

"Sage—"

"I just wanted you to know in case we don't… Just in case." She touched her cool fingertips to his cheek. "It still can be different. You have only to stop me from walking away."

He opened his mouth to say the words. They got stuck in his throat and wouldn't come out.

With a last sad look, she went to her cousin's SUV and climbed in, sitting in the seat next to Isa. He stood and watched as Roberto drove away. Sage's tear-stained face appeared briefly in the window.

The next instant, she was gone, along with a sizable chunk of Gavin's heart.

Chapter Fifteen

It hadn't taken long for the road to Powell Ranch to become familiar. As Sage drove it today, quite probably for the last time, memories came flooding back with each familiar landmark she passed.

She'd traveled this same stretch of pavement on the day she met Gavin. It was right along here that she'd told Isa about the paternity test. Leaving the valley with the mustang had been the worst memory, until today. She was bringing him back, only not to Gavin's.

So much had happened in only a few short weeks.

Damn Gavin for allowing her to leave last night. Why did she have to go and fall for such a stubborn man? Stubborn, irritating, always convinced he was right and prideful. She'd like to wring his neck with that last one.

He was also strong, dependable, honest to a fault and trustworthy. Mostly, he put his family above all others. Fine qualities in a man and the reason she'd fallen in love with him.

It was possible, in her effort to make amends for her part in him losing the mustang, she'd gone overboard and pushed too hard. Her enthusiastic suggestions had come off as criticisms. Gavin asked for time and space to work through his problems on his own terms. Instead of respecting his wishes, she'd invited her and Isa to move in with him, thrown money around, *Dan's* money at that, and suggested she and Gavin become business partners.

In hindsight, she'd been insensitive to his needs.

He hadn't exactly been sensitive to her needs, either. His rejection of her was brutal. Cruel. She hadn't deserved that even if she did unintentionally insult him.

What a mess. A stinking, miserable mess.

As if voicing his opinion on the matter, the mustang kicked the side of the trailer. The bang reverberated through the truck all the way to the cab.

"Yeah, yeah, we're almost there."

Signs for Mustang Village and the drive leading to Powell Ranch passed in a blur—from tears, not the speed at which she drove. Blinking, she removed a tissue from the travel-size box on the console and wiped rather ineffectually at her eyes.

The new owner of the mustang didn't live far. She dug around in the pile of papers beside her, searching for the one with the address and the attorney's phone number in case she got lost.

A sudden gust of wind caught the horse trailer and pushed it hard to the left. Sage compensated by twisting the steering wheel to the right. It had been like that the past sixty miles, her battling the strong winds sweeping across the highway.

More familiar landmarks prompted more memories and more regrets. Lost in thought and not paying attention, she yelped in surprise when another gust of wind grabbed her truck and shoved her over the center line. Reacting quickly, she swung the steering wheel too far to the right, causing the truck to swerve off the road. The right front tire ran over a pile of nasty-looking debris. Almost immediately, the truck began to weave.

Sage applied the brakes, careful to come to a slow rather than sudden stop so the trailer wouldn't fishtail. The truck rocked unevenly, making a loud thump, thump, thump, as she scouted for a safe place to pull off the road.

"Oh, hell," she grumbled, "I do not need this."

The trailer, which had ridden so easily behind her truck the entire time, now dragged like a two-ton anchor. When she finally came to a complete stop, the right front of the truck dipped at a sharp angle.

Under normal circumstances, she could change a flat tire with no problem. The horse trailer complicated the task considerably. She'd have to unhitch it, change out the tire, then rehitch the trailer. Not easy, but not impossible.

She peered back down the road. Powell Ranch was only a mile away. If Gavin was there, he'd come and help her. She had no doubt of it despite their awful breakup.

Taking out her cell phone, she dialed a number. Not his, the attorney's. Seeing her again, seeing the mustang, would be too difficult for Gavin, and she didn't want to put him through any more grief.

The attorney answered on the third ring, and she told him about the flat tire. He put her on hold and returned a couple minutes later, informing her his client would be there shortly and driving a white Ford crew cab pickup. She was to sit tight and wait for him. Under no circumstances was she to attempt to change the flat tire herself.

Fine. She could do that.

More than one person driving by stopped and asked if she was all right. Sage thanked them and told them help was arriving any minute.

After a while, she decided to get out and check on the mustang. Snorting at her and pawing the floor, he let her know how displeased he was about the delay and how much he disliked riding in trailers.

"Sorry, buddy, I don't like this, either."

More vehicles passed. Sage pushed her hair out of her face.

The wind instantly blew it back. When she looked up, she saw a familiar truck approaching from the direction of the ranch. As it drew closer, there was no mistaking the driver.

Gavin.

What was he doing here?

He drove slowly past her, pulled off the road in front of her and parked. She wavered between throwing herself in his arms and storming off in a huff. He opened his door, got out and strolled toward her, stopping briefly to look inside the trailer.

The mustang kicked the sidewall, his way of saying hello.

"Hi." He smiled at Sage, though it was a pretty weak one.

"Hey."

"I was on my way to the feed store."

He seemed as uncomfortable as she.

He was also hurting, it showed in his eyes.

Join the club.

"What happened?" he asked, going around to the front of the truck and examining the flat.

She came up behind him and stood a little too close. His powerful build, his height, the attraction that had flared between them right from the start, overwhelmed her, and she had to step away.

"The wind caught the trailer. I overcompensated and ran over a pile of debris." She didn't mention she'd been thinking of him when it happened. "The owner of the mustang is on his way here now," she said, hinting it might be best for him to leave.

"No reason we can't get started. Where's your jack?"

"I'm supposed to sit tight."

He ignored her. "Is it in the toolbox?" Without waiting for

her to answer, he climbed into the bed of the truck and held out his hand to her. "Key?"

Since arguing was useless, she handed him her key ring. "Think we should get the mustang out?"

He unlocked the toolbox and removed the jack. "If we do, I'm not sure we can control him with just the two of us."

Actually, there would be three of them. But who knew if the new owner was any kind of cowboy? He might have no experience with horses and purchased the mustang for other reasons.

Gavin unhitched the horse trailer and set up the jack. He'd just started pumping the handle when a white Ford pickup driving down the opposite lane slowed and then stopped.

"I think he's here," Sage said, worried at how Gavin would react to the man.

He didn't look up from his task. Not even when the truck door opened and the man stepped out. Sage recognized him instantly.

Shock coursed through her. *Impossible! It can't be him.*

He strode toward them, his gait purposeful, his cowboy hat angled low over his eyes.

She braced herself for what would surely be an ugly confrontation.

Behind her, the noise from the cranking jack stopped. The next sound she heard was Gavin swearing.

"Ms. Navarre." Clay Duvall inclined his head at Sage. "Gavin. You folks need a hand?"

"HELL, NO," GAVIN SAID CURTLY. "We don't need a hand." He didn't care if Clay Duvall now owned the mustang. The man wasn't lifting so much as a pinky to assist him and Sage.

"Where's your spare?"

"Get back in your truck, Duvall."

Duvall acted as if he hadn't heard Gavin. He went to the

rear of Sage's truck, stopping momentarily to examine the mustang. For once, the horse didn't kick or attempt to bite.

Gavin pumped the jack handle harder.

Kneeling on the ground between the truck and trailer, Duvall bent to peer at the spare tire attached to the truck's underside. "Do you have a wrench, Ms. Navarre?"

Sage started for the toolbox.

"Stay there," Gavin growled. To Duvall, he said, "I'll remove the spare."

"I'm already down here," Duvall answered pleasantly enough, though there was unmistakable tension in his voice. When no one immediately responded, he climbed back to his feet. "No problem. I have a wrench in my truck."

"You knew I wanted that horse."

Duvall stopped midstep and turned around. "You weren't the only one."

Gavin straightened. "I tracked him for months."

"And again, you weren't the only one."

Gavin was taken aback. He'd assumed only a few residents in the valley knew about the mustang and that he alone was interested in capturing him. "You have no use for that horse."

"Actually, I do." Duvall appeared remarkably calm.

Gavin, in comparison, was holding on to his control by the thinnest of threads.

"I figure with his temperament, that fellow will produce some nice offspring for my bucking stock."

"What bucking stock?"

"For my arena. And to lease out to local rodeos. I started the business six months ago. I thought you knew."

"Why would I know or care what kind of business you started?"

"Because of Ethan."

"What about him?"

"He's been helping me."

The words struck Gavin like a rain of fire. Ethan? Helping Duvall? How could his brother talk to, much less help, the son of the bastard who ruined them?

"You're lying," Gavin ground out.

"Ask him yourself."

Gavin would do more than ask Ethan when he saw him next. He'd knock him flat to the ground.

"Are you all right?" Sage's voice, soft in his ear, reached the part of his brain still functioning normally.

He should answer her. She was worried about him. Because she cared. Even after the rotten things he'd said to her last night.

"Yeah, I'm fine." Except, he wasn't.

Learning Duvall owned the mustang was bad. That he'd recruited Ethan...

Gavin couldn't take any more. The fury building inside him boiled over.

"It's not enough that you took our land and our livelihood. You have to take my brother's loyalty, too?"

"I didn't take anything from you."

Technically, Duvall was right. At least about the land and their livelihood. His father was the one to do that. But Ethan? So what if he and Duvall were once best friends? That didn't excuse Duvall going behind Gavin's back or Ethan's betrayal.

"And as far as your brother helping me," Duvall continued, "you'll have to talk to him about that."

"Oh, I will," Gavin assured him. "Count on it."

The flat tire wasn't changing itself. All of a sudden, he wanted the hell out of there. But he wouldn't abandon Sage, leave her with that slimeball.

Digging through her toolbox, he found the lug wrench and went over to the flat tire, now elevated well off the ground thanks to his furious pumping of the jack handle.

Duvall followed him, peered over Gavin's shoulder as he struggled to loosen the frozen lug nuts. "For the record, I didn't agree with what my dad did to yours."

Gavin didn't answer, taking his frustration out instead on his task. The air might have a nip to it but sweat beaded along his brow and ran down his neck.

"It's one of the reasons I haven't spoken to him in years."

Gavin paused, digested that information, then resumed loosening lug nuts. He'd heard rumors about Duvall and his father, though he didn't realize they'd become completely estranged. Not that he cared.

"You used the money you got from the sale of my family's land to bankroll your rodeo arena."

"I didn't. I used income from selling my share of the cattle business. I refused to have anything to do with my dad after he sold your family's land to the investor, including taking money from him."

Now, that was something Gavin hadn't heard.

But again, he didn't care. The hard shell surrounding his heart wouldn't let him forgive any of the Duvalls or feel sorry for their troubles.

He felt it then, Sage's hand on his shoulder. Warm. Soft. Gentle. Offering him her unspoken support. Letting him know she was there for him.

It was what he'd wanted from her last night, what he needed now, today, more than ever.

When this was over and Duvall had left, he was telling Sage he loved her. What she'd said was true. They could build a future together. Everything didn't need to be in place first.

"You and your family weren't the only ones who suffered at the hands of my father," Duvall said.

Gavin stood, Sage still by his side. His feelings for her might have changed his thinking, but they hadn't affected his anger at Duvall one tiny bit.

"Maybe not. But you still have your money and your rodeo arena. And now you have my brother's loyalty and my horse. What else of mine do you want, Duvall?"

"Your friendship."

"That will never happen."

"Why the hell not?" The question erupted from Sage's mouth, the corners of which turned down in an impatient frown.

Both men stared at her, Gavin in confusion and Duvall in mild amusement.

"Sage, you don't understand—"

"I do," she interrupted. "I understand perfectly. This man's father did a terrible thing to your family." She pointed to Duvall. "Not him, his father. When he was what? Nineteen? Twenty? All right, fine. You've held him accountable. Blamed him for his father's actions. Angry people do that. But the man's trying to apologize, for pity's sake. The least you can do is listen to him. Ethan obviously did."

"Don't compare me to Ethan."

If she heard Gavin, she paid no attention. "Your brother's been able to put his anger aside in order to help Mr. Duvall at whatever it is they're doing. If you weren't so pigheaded—" she jabbed a finger in Gavin's chest "—you'd realize you could work with him, too."

"Are you crazy?"

"A little, I suppose. But sometimes, crazy ideas are the best ones. He has the mustang. You have the mares. Seems to me you could strike up a partnership. Can't be any worse than the one you had with Dan."

The idea was preposterous. Insane.

Gavin glanced at Duvall, who shrugged.

Was he actually considering it?

Should Gavin?

"I really only want to breed him," Duvall said. "Don't need

him on my property. He could just as easily stay at your place. And I could bring my mares there. If you ever finish building that mare motel."

Ethan must have told Duvall about their plans.

They could get started on the construction right away, using the money they'd pooled to buy the mustang. It would be a risk but when didn't gain require risk?

There was only one drawback. He'd be betting everything that Duvall wasn't cut from the same cloth as his father.

Gavin gazed at Sage, taking in the features of her lovely face. Something inside his chest shifted. It was, he realized, the hard shell surrounding his heart melting.

She smiled, her eyes telling him, *Take the leap. I'll be with you the whole way.*

"Okay," Gavin said, and did something he wouldn't have believed possible in a million years. He extended his hand to Duvall. "We have a deal."

Duvall shook Gavin's hand firmly. "Good."

"We'll write up the agreement later."

"I'm not worried about it." Duvall grinned. "Let's find that wrench and get this gal of yours on the road."

"Think you can turn this truck and trailer around?" Duvall asked Sage when they were done changing the flat tire. "Take that horse to Powell Ranch?"

So, Gavin thought, Duvall meant what he'd said. He was letting Gavin take the mustang home.

"Piece of cake." Sage jumped into her truck after saying goodbye to Duvall.

The two men watched her head down the road.

"She's something else," Duvall said. "If I were you, I'd grab her up before another man does."

Gavin thought that was pretty good advice.

"You want to come by tomorrow for supper?" The spontaneous invitation appeared to surprise Duvall as much as it did Gavin.

"What time?"

"Six o'clock. Bring your whole family."

They shook hands again, then started toward their trucks. "Clay," Gavin called after him.

"Yeah?"

"Thanks."

Clay touched the brim of his hat, checked oncoming traffic and jogged across the street.

Cresting the top of the long drive, Gavin studied the ranch with fresh eyes. The house, the grounds, the barn and stables might be in need of repair, but they were strong and solid and built to weather the worst storms. Like his family. Like him.

He would fix the place up. A little at a time in the Powell tradition. For Cassie and Sage, too. If she'd have him.

He found her behind the old cattle barn, soon to be the new mare motel.

"I wasn't sure where you wanted to put him up tonight," she said, meeting up with Gavin at the rear of the trailer.

"I'm not sure, either." He unlatched the trailer door. "Let's see what kind of mood he's in."

The mustang backed out, not charged out, as was his customary exit. And rather than fight the lead rope, he stood, surveying his newly permanent surroundings. With a satisfied snort, he lowered his head and bumped Gavin's arm in what could be considered affection. At least, that was what Gavin chose to believe.

Sage laughed. "I think he's happy."

"He's not the only one."

Over in the pasture, Avaro whinnied. The mustang turned to look at her, his regal head raised high in the air. The other mares bunched together at the fence. He was special. They knew it, and he knew it.

"*Principe*," Sage said.

Gavin spoke enough Spanish to recognize the word. "Prince. That's a good name for him. Prince of the McDowell Mountains."

"I'm happy for you, Gavin."

With his free arm he hooked her by the waist and hauled her against him. Both she and the mustang were startled by the abrupt move. Both also quickly settled, Sage into Gavin's embrace.

"I've been an idiot the last couple of days."

"Glad you came to your senses."

"If not for you, I wouldn't have Prince."

"You'd have caught him on your own eventually."

"No, I mean now. Your idea that Clay and I become partners, it was…"

"Genius."

"Half-genius." He bent and brushed her lips with his.

"What?" She withdrew, feigning insult.

He pulled her back into his arms. "Clay will make a great business partner. I have someone else in mind for my *life* partner."

"Are you sure?" she asked hesitantly.

"Move to Mustang Valley. You and Isa. Marry me. Make this rambling old place into a home again. I know it won't always be easy. I can be stubborn sometimes."

"Sometimes?" she chided.

"I love you, Sage."

She repeated the sentiment, in a whisper against his lips, right before she accepted his proposal with a kiss.

Epilogue

Three months later

Gavin and Sage sat in the courtyard on chairs his father had built for his grandparents, enjoying the view and each other's company. They held hands, as was typical when the two of them were within touching distance. Sunlight poured through the branches of the trimmed trees and glistened off the water trickling down the center column of the fountain.

Those weren't the only changes around the Powell house.

At Gavin's urging, Sage and Isa had moved in. They'd done so shortly after she started her new job with the Game and Fish Department. At the same time, Ethan moved out, though he went only as far as the old bunkhouse behind the barn. The weekend warriors who were helping them construct the mare motel, all friends and neighbors, including Clay Duvall, also lent their talented manpower to converting the bunkhouse into a cozy apartment.

Isa had her own bedroom, as did Cassie. She'd returned to Connecticut for the two weeks over Christmas, then flew home early January right before school started. Gavin hadn't known when he put her on the plane if she'd be back. Cassie had called him Christmas day to deliver the good news. Next to Sage setting a wedding date for May seventh, it was the best present he'd received.

That left one empty bedroom in the house. Gavin thought it might make a nice nursery when they were ready to add to the family. Next year, maybe. When Sage was more settled in her new job, the stud and breeding business operating solidly in the black and the wild mustang sanctuary they were starting this spring fully operational.

Prince, as everyone called him, was still a handful but he knew his job on the ranch and did it well. Nine mares were already carrying his offspring, one of them Avaro. Ethan continued the task of training Prince—when he wasn't teaching riding classes or breaking horses. Dan and his family left Mustang Valley and moved to Casa Grande. Ethan, the only other experienced horse trainer in the area, had picked up many of Dan's former clients.

As far as Gavin knew, no one missed Dan. Certainly not he and Sage. As long as the child support payments came like clockwork, he hoped to never see the man again. Sage, of course, had left the door open for him to visit Isa. Maybe someday he'd realize what a treasure he had in the little girl. Well, his loss was Gavin's gain.

Bringing Sage's hand to his lips, he kissed the sensitive skin at her wrist.

"I was thinking," she said wistfully, her gaze taking in the view of the valley below. "The courtyard might make a great place for the wedding ceremony. Late afternoon. When the sun is just setting."

"Sounds good to me."

"Anna offered to lend me her dress."

He imagined Sage in a white wedding gown and coming down the steps into the courtyard. The picture made him smile, as did the small, precious item he carried in his pocket.

"I guess that's everything," he said.

"All the important stuff."

"Except for one." He reached in his pocket and pulled out a diamond-and-emerald ring. "My father gave me this today."

Sage gasped.

"It belonged to my mother. Dad said he'd be honored if you wore it." Gavin got out of the chair and went down on one knee in front of Sage. "So would I. Deeply honored."

"Oh, Gavin. Yes!" She extended her left hand for him to place the ring on her finger. "It's beautiful. I love it. I love you."

He stood and pulled her to her feet, sealing their now official engagement with a kiss that conveyed everything in his heart more than words ever could.

As they walked into the house to show off the ring to the rest of the family, Gavin swore he could feel the presence of his grandfather and great-grandfather. In the pictures that hung in the hallway. In the tiles beneath their feet. In the walls that had sheltered and protected five generations of Powells—and would continue to for many more generations to come.

* * * * *

Ethan's story is next in Cathy McDavid's
MUSTANG VALLEY *miniseries.*
Coming soon, only from
Harlequin American Romance.

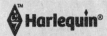

Harlequin®

American ★ Romance®

COMING NEXT MONTH

Available September 13, 2011

#1369 MONTANA SHERIFF
American Romance's Men of the West
Marie Ferrarella

#1370 THE BULL RIDER'S TWINS
Callahan Cowboys
Tina Leonard

#1371 STAND-IN MOM
Creature Comforts
Megan Kelly

#1372 BACHELOR DAD
Fatherhood
Roxann Delaney

You can find more information on upcoming
Harlequin® titles, free excerpts and more at
www.HarlequinInsideRomance.com.

HARCNM0811

REQUEST YOUR FREE BOOKS!
2 FREE NOVELS PLUS 2 FREE GIFTS!

Harlequin

American ★ Romance®
LOVE, HOME & HAPPINESS

YES! Please send me 2 FREE Harlequin® American Romance® novels and my 2 FREE gifts (gifts are worth about $10). After receiving them, if I don't wish to receive any more books, I can return the shipping statement marked "cancel." If I don't cancel, I will receive 4 brand-new novels every month and be billed just $4.49 per book in the U.S. or $5.24 per book in Canada. That's a saving of at least 14% off the cover price! It's quite a bargain! Shipping and handling is just 50¢ per book in the U.S. and 75¢ per book in Canada.* I understand that accepting the 2 free books and gifts places me under no obligation to buy anything. I can always return a shipment and cancel at any time. Even if I never buy another book, the two free books and gifts are mine to keep forever.

154/354 HDN FEP2

Name _____ (PLEASE PRINT)

Address _____ Apt. #

City _____ State/Prov. _____ Zip/Postal Code

Signature (if under 18, a parent or guardian must sign)

Mail to the Reader Service:
IN U.S.A.: P.O. Box 1867, Buffalo, NY 14240-1867
IN CANADA: P.O. Box 609, Fort Erie, Ontario L2A 5X3

Not valid for current subscribers to Harlequin American Romance books.

Want to try two free books from another line?
Call 1-800-873-8635 or visit www.ReaderService.com.

* Terms and prices subject to change without notice. Prices do not include applicable taxes. Sales tax applicable in N.Y. Canadian residents will be charged applicable taxes. Offer not valid in Quebec. This offer is limited to one order per household. All orders subject to credit approval. Credit or debit balances in a customer's account(s) may be offset by any other outstanding balance owed by or to the customer. Please allow 4 to 6 weeks for delivery. Offer available while quantities last.

Your Privacy—The Reader Service is committed to protecting your privacy. Our Privacy Policy is available online at www.ReaderService.com or upon request from the Reader Service.

We make a portion of our mailing list available to reputable third parties that offer products we believe may interest you. If you prefer that we not exchange your name with third parties, or if you wish to clarify or modify your communication preferences, please visit us at www.ReaderService.com/consumerschoice or write to us at Reader Service Preference Service, P.O. Box 9062, Buffalo, NY 14269. Include your complete name and address.

HARI1B

New York Times *and* USA TODAY *bestselling author*
Maya Banks presents a brand-new miniseries

PREGNANCY & PASSION

When four irresistible tycoons face
the consequences of temptation.

Book 1—ENTICED BY HIS FORGOTTEN LOVER

Available September 2011 from Harlequin® Desire®!

Rafael de Luca had been in bad situations before. A crowded ballroom could never make him sweat.

These people would never know that he had no memory of any of them.

He surveyed the party with grim tolerance, searching for the source of his unease.

At first his gaze flickered past her, but he yanked his attention back to a woman across the room. Her stare bored holes through him. Unflinching and steady, even when his eyes locked with hers.

Petite, even in heels, she had a creamy olive complexion. A wealth of inky-black curls cascaded over her shoulders and her eyes were equally dark.

She looked at him as if she'd already judged him and found him lacking. He'd never seen her before in his life. Or had he?

He cursed the gaping hole in his memory. He'd been diagnosed with selective amnesia after his accident four months ago. Which seemed like complete and utter bull. No one got amnesia except hysterical women in bad soap operas.

With a smile, he disengaged himself from the group

around him and made his way to the mystery woman.

She wasn't coy. She stared straight at him as he approached, her chin thrust upward in defiance.

"Excuse me, but have we met?" he asked in his smoothest voice.

His gaze moved over the generous swell of her breasts pushed up by the empire waist of her black cocktail dress.

When he glanced back up at her face, he saw fury in her eyes.

"Have we *met?*" Her voice was barely a whisper, but he felt each word like the crack of a whip.

Before he could process her response, she nailed him with a right hook. He stumbled back, holding his nose.

One of his guards stepped between Rafe and the woman, accidentally sending her to one knee. Her hand flew to the folds of her dress.

It was then, as she cupped her belly, that the realization hit him. She was pregnant.

Her eyes flashing, she turned and ran down the marble hallway.

Rafael ran after her. He burst from the hotel lobby, and saw two shoes sparkling in the moonlight, twinkling at him.

He blew out his breath in frustration and then shoved the pair of sparkly, ultrafeminine heels at his head of security.

"Find the woman who wore these shoes."

Will Rafael find his mystery woman?
Find out in Maya Banks's passionate new novel
ENTICED BY HIS FORGOTTEN LOVER
Available September 2011 from Harlequin® Desire®!

Harlequin®

ROMANTIC
SUSPENSE

NEW YORK TIMES BESTSELLING AUTHOR
RACHEL LEE

The Rescue Pilot

Time is running out…

Desperate to help her ailing sister, Rory is determined
to get Cait the necessary treatment to help her fight
a devastating disease. A cross-country trip turns into
a fight for survival in more ways than one when their plane
encounters trouble. Can Rory trust pilot Chase Dakota
with their lives, and possibly her heart?

**Look for this heart-stopping romance in September
from *New York Times* bestselling author Rachel Lee
and Harlequin Romantic Suspense!**

Conard County THE NEXT GENERATION

Available in September wherever books are sold!

www.Harlequin.com.

RSRL27741